CERRIE BURNELL

The Ice Bear Miracle

OXFORD
UNIVERSITY PRESS

For Amelie, my fairy tale girl

OXFORD
UNIVERSITY PRESS

Great Clarendon Street, Oxford OX2 6DP
Oxford University Press is a department of the University of Oxford.
It furthers the University's objective of excellence in research, scholarship,
and education by publishing worldwide. Oxford is a registered trade mark
of Oxford University Press in the UK and in certain other countries

Database right Oxford University Press (maker)

First published 2020

British Library Cataloguing in Publication Data

Data available

ISBN: 978-019-276756-1

1 3 5 7 9 10 8 6 4 2

Printed in Great Britain

Paper used in the production of this book is a natural,
recyclable product made from wood grown in sustainable forests.
The manufacturing process conforms to the environmental
regulations of the country of origin.

Chapter 1

LIFE WITH BEARS

Somewhere off the coast of Canada, in the deep and frozen north, is an island surrounded entirely by ice. It is not the kind of ice you will ever have known. It is luminous and strange, and there are lost things trapped forever inside it. The fin of an orca. A baby's boot. The figurehead of a ship.

In late spring some of the ice melts, giving way to a cold and wondrous sea. And from May till August the ice is no more than a whisper, glimpsed only on the surface of the island's rare, frost-glittered lake. But in autumn the sea begins to slow and freeze, taking its time, until not a single green wave is left. As the leaves on the island turn orange and gold and the nights lengthen to days of winter dark, that is when the bears come. Giants the colour of snow, lumbering in packs, rolling in on silent paws. Their eyes hungry and bright, snouts sniffing at the crisp pale air.

The folk who live on the Isle of Bears are proud of its name and history. They love their ice-locked island, with its scattered wooden cottages, its small patches of Canadian forest, its rushing River Raven and its single mountain peak, upon which there is a sparkling lake that's always frozen. They love how even in summer you can skate on Lake Rarity and play hockey by the light of the faint Arctic moon. Or how in winter hundreds of visitors from far, unheard of places, pass through the town, taking refuge from storms or calling in on friends before they head further north. When the first snow falls, the townsfolk leave their doors unlocked and hearts open to welcome everyone. They light fires and head home early to drink hot chocolate and sing songs of ice legends and whisper winter myths, while beyond their windows white bears roam the streets.

Polar bear migration is what the scientists and environmentalists call it, but the islanders call it LIFE WITH BEARS and it's their greatest joy.

There are many dark and light stories on an island like this. Marv Jackson knew all about it. For what had happened to Marv on the River Raven on the night of his fifth birthday was not a story he would ever forget.

It was the kind of tale that worked its way into even the toughest heart, so wherever Marv went, the story preceded him, and he was known as the boy who fought a bear—and lived to see the sunrise. Though that wasn't what had happened at all. But still people chose to think of him as a child cut from courage and hope, and quietly, they began to call him Marvel.

The story according to the islanders went something like this:

On a cold and treacherous midwinter night Marv crept into his garden. He was new to the Isle of Bears. His family had come from Toronto—they hadn't been here more than a year. They were still adjusting to this wild, wintered island, so different from the city, full of starry darkness, mystery, wonder. Still learning its songs and late-night tales. Still getting to know its kind, hardy people.

Sure Marv knew the rules. It's the first thing the Polar Patrol officers tell you, the moment you step off the plane.

o *Don't go out after nightfall.*

o *Never leave the house alone in a snowstorm.*

o *If you stumble upon a bear, never look it in the eye—get to shelter.*

But he was only five, with an eager heart and eagle eye. No—he wasn't a trouble-seeker. He was simply a child drawn to the ice, like a ship to a star.

Marv was dressed from head to toe in his hockey kit, including, thankfully, the helmet. He crept out of his garden, stick in hand, skates laced loosely around his ankles, puck heavy in his pocket. And headed straight for the River Raven, which if he'd followed south with a midnight wind at his back, would have led him to the Island's smallest lake: Lake Clarity. A sheltered little lake, no bigger than a large pond, where two larch trees had bent beneath the weight of snow to form a natural hockey net.

But Marv didn't reach Lake Clarity. The bear appeared on the River Raven, seized the child in its wintered mouth, raised him into the air. Marv yelled out, and both his family and many of the neighbours and winter visitors came running, hurling anything they could at the bear. China bowls, a broken chair, a single slipper. But the bear only raged into a deeper fury.

Somehow in the midst of the horror Marv managed to strike the bear in the eye with his hockey stick. Not enough to harm her, but just enough to stun her. For a moment the bear stilled, and Old Stoney shot at her—the bullet, like a dart of silver fire, grazed her sleek fur and pinged off a car. The bear dropped Marv and the crowd rushed in and saved his life.

That's how Marv became Marvel. He got away with his life, got a scar to mark his adventure. And you know what else? He got real good at hockey.

Marv had long stopped trying to convince anyone else outside his home that things had been different; it was easier to let them have their fairy tale.

What Marv remembered was this. It was his birthday—and his first-ever time at training. His Dad

4

had bought him all the hockey kit as a present. And Coach, their trusted family friend, had been there throughout, holding the hockey stick horizontally for Marv to clutch as he wobbled joyfully around the rink. He'd been so happy that when he had got home and blown out his flickering candles, he'd fallen asleep on the couch refusing to take any of the kit off.

He awoke to the sound of a baby crying.

The house was in darkness, the gleam of the streetlamp streaming in, making the frosted windows look like spun sugar. Looking up through the cage-like guard of his helmet, Marv noticed the digital clock in the hallway said 11.50. He didn't know what the numbers meant, but he remembered them.

The sound came again, a little yelping cry that burrowed straight into his soul. Marv stumbled blindly toward the back door, pressing his ear to it through the helmet. Like every back door on the island it was unlocked in case someone needed to escape from a bear. Or a traveller arriving late at night needed refuge.

The handle turned easily in Marv's small gloved hand and he peered out into the star-scattered night. A winter gale whistled past his éars and Marv shivered. In the near distance the baby gave an angry screech. Clutching his hockey stick to his heart Marv clambered out.

o   *Don't go out after nightfall.*

🌲 5 🌲

A million snowflakes whirled through his visor, kissing his eyelashes and nipping at his cheeks. The wail of the baby became like an eerie lullaby, drawing Marv through the snowfall, out of his garden, across the deserted street to the banks of the River Raven. Thick ice mirrored the thunder-coloured sky, and tiny speckles of starlight glinted off it like magic. And there in the centre of the river, like a present fallen from a flying sleigh, was a wicker basket holding a restless crying baby.

Marv stood still, hypnotized by the odd wonder of the little scene. The strangeness of it felt like a moment out of time, as if midnight had ceased its chimes for the boy and the baby.

A large moon-bright snowflake blotted out Marv's vision and the baby's cry became his whole existence. A silvery thread sewn from sound, which knotted around him, pulling him forward. Even as the wind shrieked around him and fresh snow shuddered down from the sky, Marv edged forward.

o   *Never leave the house alone in a snowstorm.*

It was too late for that now . . . Marv didn't think. He put his blades on the ice and using his stick to steady himself, wobbled uncertainly onto the night river. Twice he fell and clambered back up, his skates tied so loosely they dragged instead of glided.

The River Raven was much wider than it looked.

Marv felt like he was crossing an ocean, one unbalanced slide at a time. He was five or six steps from the basket when he felt the weight of watchful eyes.

o   *If you stumble upon a bear, never look it in the eye—
    get to shelter.*

Marv looked up straight into the gaze of the most astounding little snout-nosed face he'd ever seen. It nearly stole all his breath away. A wonderfully sweet cub with eyes like the forest at midnight was scampering toward him. The cub skidded here and pounced there, playful as a kitten. He chomped his sharp-toothed mouth at a drifting flake, did a tumbling roll, then began spinning around on his tummy like a furry starfish, and Marv couldn't help grinning.

The baby howled and kicked crossly. The cub blinked in the starlight, turning its small black snout toward the sound. With a little shake of his head, the cub scrambled up and bounded gleefully toward the babe. Marv felt a beat of worry pulse through him. Ever so slowly he shuffled himself around, so he was between the basket and the cub, stealing a glance at the wriggling child inside as he did.

She was small and absolutely savage with rage. A halo of black curls framed her furious face, while she pummelled her woollen blanket with maddened fists, her tiny feet kicking at snowflakes, one in a pink boot, one in only a little sock. Marv thought she looked far more feral than the bear cub. And yet, as he stared, he found there was something captivating about her. Her skin was the same autumn brown as Marv's own, and her eyes when she finally stared at him were endlessly deep like the dark between stars.

Nothing would stop her from living. Not the north winds, nor the mountains, nor the hunger of hunting bears. This child was demanding to be part of the universe, and the universe would simply have to listen. It would brighten its moon, untether its seasons, alter its stars for her.

The ice on the River Raven creaked and the night air seemed suddenly to smell of blood. Again Marv had the swift and chilling sense of being watched. He tilted his head ever so slightly, trying to peer out through the side of his helmet, and there on the horizon he caught sight of a monstrous shadow. A mama bear! She was the same Arctic shape as her cub only much, much bigger, as if crafted from wilderness and claws.

But she was far enough away that Marv had time. He just had to stay calm, and move slowly.

Only he couldn't just leave the baby.

Somehow he found himself sliding toward the howling baby, his skates slipping in all directions, his balance a gamble between life and death. He crouched down to try and lift the basket, but almost fell and squashed the baby! It was just too slippery on the ice. So he shoved the basket lightly with his hockey stick and watched it glide easily down the River Raven and into a thicket of bilberry bushes. The baby was cloaked in shadows, almost invisible but for her cries. Marv tripped and traipsed after her, but his skates were slowing him down. He'd leave her there—she was hidden enough— and get help from home.

Then he thought he saw a figure on the ice in a long winter coat. He breathed a short sigh of relief. Help was here. The baby would be safe.

He began to scramble back toward the snowy bank when there came a roar that could shatter bones. That was when Marv realized how close the mama bear was. Too close, and suddenly he was trembling with fear.

And here Marv's memory seemed to have frozen. Perhaps he'd passed out and fallen into the bear's violent jaws. Perhaps his soul slipped from his body and drifted up to the trees ready to become stardust, or perhaps the terror of the attack was just too damaging to relive. Because the next thing Marv remembered was the sensation of flying, as a huge bear swung him side to side.

Marv forgot the baby and wintry figure and bellowed for his mom.

One moment the River Raven was empty and it was him, the moon, and the bear. The next it was crowded with people. He heard his mother's screams splintering the night. He saw a single slipper sailing past him. He glimpsed the barrel of a loaded gun. He grabbed his hockey stick in both hands and shoved it backwards, striking something soft. The world went still. The crack of a gunshot deafened Marv and the cool ice kissed him as he fell from the bear's mouth.

When Marv finally opened his eyes he was at the small island hospital, which was no bigger than a house. His parents were both clinging to each other and quietly weeping. Doctor Marilee was smiling at him, though her eyes looked tired.

'Is the baby OK?' Marv tried to say, though the stitches tugged at his mouth and eye where he would be marked forever by a crescent moon scar. Nobody answered. They had thought Marv delirious.

What baby? There was no one but you on the ice . . .

Marv tried to tell the story again and again, but no one could ever help him. None of the townsfolk, or the winter tourists, or any late-night travellers had seen anything.

You must have heard the whistle of the wind. Imagined it was a baby.

As the years went by the memory became hazy. Yet sometimes Marv dreamed of a girl with brown skin and jewel-bright eyes, living with a winter-white bear, dancing beneath the northern sky, adorned in a pink blanket that she wore like a cape, and he could never quite let go of the hope it was the baby. For deep down in the most secretive chamber of his heart, Marv knew there had been a child. A child who had demanded to live.

Chapter 2

AUTUMN ON THE ISLE OF BEARS

Marv sat up and shivered hard, pushing back his green curtains and gazing out onto the Jacksons' small, ramshackle yard. Pale sunshine kissed the petals of vivid flowers, but the wind tugged swiftly at the grass. Seven, nearly eight years had passed since the bear attack, but still every time Marv felt summer slip swiftly into autumn, his memories of that night awoke, and he found himself dreaming more of the girl, and wondering about the mama bear, who had given him his scar. Would he see her again? Would she come back to the island this year? For she was still out there wandering the Arctic as if searching for something that she lost long ago.

Marv hopped out of bed and pulled on a pair of hockey socks, blinking at the coldness which swept through his room. It was early September but already the air tasted of snow.

This'll make Mom happy. A proper winter, with thick ice.

Everyone on the island lived for ice. And everyone was gravely concerned that each year the sea froze later and later. Marv's mom, Indi, was more troubled than most, as part of her role at the research centre was to study climate change and try to protect the island from ice melt—and the bears from going hungry.

Marv wriggled into his jeans and slipped on an oversized hoody, excited by the thought of the river and sea freezing earlier. It meant more skating by twilight, more deep snowfall, more hunting time for the bears.

Marv at once felt hugely hopeful.

Winter's going to be awesome!

He glanced in the mirror, lowering his hood: dark eyes flecked with green peered back at him. Brown skin marked forever by a silver scar. Marv grabbed his favourite cap and tried to flatten his untamed hair with it.

He pretty much wore the cap everywhere he went. It was faded burgundy with his team's logo depicted in gold thread: a single mountain peak with a polar bear raising its nose to the moon. The team's name *The Ice Bear Miracles* had once been stitched beneath it, but the thread had unravelled over time. He pulled the last of it away and bounded downstairs, helping himself to a piece of French toast from the stack on top of the oven.

'Don't sit up there honey, sit at the table,' came Indi's voice from the corner. It was the last Saturday before school started, but Indi always rose early, to go jogging round the island, checking on her plants and experiments, popping to the research centre even on her days off.

'It feels cold Mom,' said Marv, remaining on the counter—his favourite place to sit—and flashing his mom a playful grin.

Indi raised her eyes from the article she was studying. 'It does,' she said, finally giving into her son's quiet charm. Marv couldn't see it, but his smile was the loveliest thing about him. There was so much joy in it. A lopsided little grin that pulled up higher on the scarred side of his face and filled the world with light.

The kitchen door burst dramatically open and Mya came scooting across the floor in her slippers. 'Marv, did you finish the syrup again?' she cried.

'Nope.'

Mya glared at the almost empty glass bottle. 'That's not enough for anyone. Mom, tell him not to be such a greedy little cub.'

Marv gave a loud fake yell and mimed being greatly injured as Mya punched him on the arm.

Indi did not smile. There were some things she would never smile about; one was her son being likened to a bear.

Indi had made her peace with the bear attack, of course. The Jacksons had come to the Isle of Bears for her work, a brilliant and challenging research post studying bear behaviour. Leon, Marv's dad had been enchanted by the idea of living in the wilderness, almost off-grid. A place where many northern cultures crossed paths, and everyone belonged. But they had stayed for the island. For the friends who rushed to hold them when they were afraid, for the neighbours who rescued Marv, for the doctor who carefully stitched their son back together and told them in a voice as gentle as snowflakes: 'The wound is the place where the light gets in.' And for wild winter nights where the community came together to sing and laugh and weep in wonder of this strange, miraculous place they called home.

'I expect there's more syrup in the fridge,' said Indi, rolling her eyes at her wrestling children. Mya was almost two years older than Marv but believed herself to be a lot more sophisticated. She had the same wavy dark hair and brown skin as her brother. But her eyes had more green in them, like Indi's, whereas Marv's were mostly brown the same as Leon's. Mya was several inches taller than Marv and wore her confidence like a snowflake-glittered robe, while Marv tended to keep his gaze low. And then, of course, there was the scar.

Mya called it his moon mark. She'd been nearly seven

when it happened but she remembered the horror of that night and how the next day at school she was no longer Mya Jackson, that girl from Toronto. She was Mya Jackson, sister of a bear fighter.

'Get me the syrup!' she screamed, shoving Marv to the floor.

'I can't move! My leg's completely broken,' Marv insisted.

Mya grabbed Marv's cap, and put it on backwards so the peak covered her neck. She thrust her hands deep into her dressing gown pockets and began stomping heavily about the kitchen. 'That leg's not broken!' she growled in a rough voice. 'You're an Ice Bear Miracle— now get up and play!' Even Indi began laughing. Mya had a particular knack for imitating Coach.

All the kids on the island loved Coach with a fighting pride, and spent many hours impersonating him. The Jacksons knew him better than most—he had been so welcoming when they arrived, he felt more like family than their coach. That was how Mya, who had never had any interest in hockey, nor even been coached by him, had managed to capture him just right.

Leon Jackson put his head round the door. 'Can't you take it outside?' he muttered, his voice thick with sleep from the late shift at the airport.

'Dad! You're up!' screamed Mya, skidding across the kitchen and flinging herself into his arms.

'I am now,' grumbled Leon.

'Honey, go back to bed. Kids—enough noise already. You've woken your Dad up—again!' But neither child was listening.

'Hey Dad,' said Marv, settling back on the counter.

'Hey son,' croaked Leon, ruffling the boy's hair. Marv loved it when his dad was up early at the weekend. It felt like a treat. During the week Leon worked late at the airport and was often asleep when Marv set off for school. He was a man well suited to winter, Marv often thought, content in the endless dark, at peace with the moon. Leon had never missed a hockey game though, and sometimes he came to training, hanging out with Coach and offering encouragement.

Mya squished up on the counter beside Marv.

'Both of you get down,' Indi sighed. Neither of them moved.

The counter creaked heavily beneath their weight and Leon frowned. 'Better listen to your mo—' he began, but both brother and sister tumbled to the floor, tugging him with them, and bursting out laughing. Indi rolled her eyes and went to get more syrup.

Half an hour later, Marv opened the back door and picked his way across the garden to grab his kit for training. Their white wood home with its sky-blue roof and matching doors was set a little way up a sloping hill, and the garden, which was no bigger than a yard, slanted away from the back door at funny angles. It was full of unexpected things that Marv had to cut a path around. An old wooden crate they used as a bench. Half of a rusted snowmobile. A swing that both Marv and Mya had outgrown, though on nights when the dream woke him, Marv liked to perch on it and wait for the summer moon to creep through the fleeting dark.

He reached the shed with its broken door and slipped inside. Piles and piles of the Jacksons' snow gear was crammed into every space: skis, boots, snowboards, a sledge, a million scarves, hats, and gloves, and heaped upon every surface were skates upon skates upon skates. The Jacksons' skate collection had begun when they arrived from Toronto, and was small compared to some of their neighbours.

Marv fished out his hockey gear—which Indi refused to have in the house because of the smell—checked his kit bag, then with a movement that was so automatic he could have done it with his eyes shut, he slung the bag on his back, skates across his shoulders, angled his cap down, grabbed his hockey stick, and set off for the rink taking the long route.

He had plenty of time to get there—and also Marv didn't fancy running into Kobi Stone. He and Kobi had a long-standing rivalry; Marv had lost a milk tooth to Kobi's fist when he was seven. And been 'accidentally' tripped up by him countless times on the ice. That was before Marv got fast, so fast no one could ever catch him.

Marv hadn't seen Kobi all summer. Hockey season ran through the winter months, and though the rink was always open, Marv and his best friend Sol and a few of their teammates practised outside on Lake Rarity, the island's miraculous mountain top lake, skating late into the pale northern nights.

Marv's street ran parallel to the River Raven, and as he climbed up the hill, the houses thinned out and were replaced by patches of wind-stunted forest.

Autumn on the Isle of Bears had its own strange splendour; the way the trees were adorned in the most fabulous colours moments before the wind tore the leaves away. *Autumn is when the island shows its heart* his mom always said, and as Marv breathed in the crisp mountain air, he could see what she meant.

It was then that he had the creeping sensation of being watched. He snapped his head left and right, trying to feel through the air around him, to pick up where the gaze was coming from. It was far too early for ice bears, but there were many other wild things on the island that might be watching him.

Ever since the bear attack, or maybe even before, he'd become hyper-alert to the world around him. It was one of the things that made him an excellent hockey player. He was aware of everything. All the time.

As he cut through the amber-gold forest, Marv thought he heard a twig crunch behind him, but there was no one there, so he pushed on, taking his time. He paused to peer through a gap in the woods at the view of Mount Maplewood, the island's only real mountain, named after the thicket of sugar maples that grew at its summit. The trees shouldn't have been able to survive here, but they did anyway. The island was full of wonders like that. The frozen lake at the top of Mount Maplewood. The Ice Bears.

Somewhere far behind Marv came the gentlest stirring of leaves. Marv span around, cap pushed back, staring intently into the trees.

'Hey Marvel,' came a voice from somewhere far off.

'Hey?' he answered, as a tall man stepped out of a clearing, axe in hand, a black dog with yellow eyes at his ankles.

All Marv saw was his shadow stretching out before him, yet he recognized the voice and smiled. It was Trucker, one of the woods-folk.

The woods-folk, or forest-folk, were exactly as they sounded: individuals or families who chose to live in isolated cottages, scattered throughout the woods.

'Off to training?' asked Trucker. Marv nodded. 'Got time for a hot chocolate? Rae would love to say hi.'

Marv gave a slow grin, he'd left the house early enough—he had time. They set off together through the trees, the darker-than-night dog leading the way. Rae was in Mya's year at school, but Marv knew her pretty well too as the Jacksons were Rae's snowstorm family: the house she went to when the weather was too bad to get home in. Trucker's shack was cosy and small, and strung with a row of colourful lanterns, twined with winter-flowering plants.

Marv settled down on a log as Trucker melted chocolate into tin mugs over a little crackling fire. Trucker's partner Juniper was away visiting family in Russia, but Rae came out and added some milk, giving some to the dog. Marv noticed the animal's eyes were bright like the moon and realized she was part wild.

All three of them perched on the log in an easy, leafy silence. The scent of wonderfully sweet chocolate curled up through the trees.

'Tastes like snow,' said Trucker sucking in air as if he were inhaling smoke.

Trucker would know thought Marv, as he'd got his nickname from being an ice road trucker, driving in the harshest conditions. He used to pack up his family and bring them with him, but now Rae was at school, she and Juniper tended to stay on the island.

'We'll have early snowfall, like we used to,' Rae said softly, and she turned to Marv, an inquisitive gleam in her eyes. 'Does your bear still come and see you?' Marv gave a firm nod. Rae had been at the Jacksons' house once on Marv's birthday, when the mama bear had returned to sing her soulful song outside Marv's window. It happened every year. The same bear, with her silver bullet scar, came calmly and in peace. 'It's like she's mourning something,' said Rae.

'Yeah,' Marv agreed, 'or trying to say sorry.'

Trucker grinned. 'That's the spirit Marvel. Those bears are far brighter than we give them credit for.'

Marv finished his hot chocolate and went on his way. It was such a comfort to be able to speak so openly about his bear to someone beyond his family. Trucker, Juniper, and Rae made up the few folk who had never doubted him about the baby. They knew that northern nights kept many secrets, and the ice held many myths. So they listened quietly and gave Marv hot chocolate and told him stories of the Nevkians, a legend all islanders loved to tell:

Warriors made of snow with glowing eyes. Who only appear during winter and are said to share souls with bears.

Marv found the Nevkian myths strangely heartening. There were many different stories, tales of fierce women who could soothe an angry bear with a song, or appear if a bear was in danger and freeze bear hunters to death with arrows of ice. And one about a Nevkian mother whose soul was paired with such an aggressive bear that she left her snow-child with a mortal family until the girl had grown tall and enchanting. Then she came back at the first frost to claim her.

It was that myth in particular that clung to Marv like mist, even though he knew the baby he had found on the River Raven had been real, and not cut from ice.

And no matter how many winters past, Marv knew, he just *knew*, she was out there.

Chapter 3

TUESDAY

As Marv made his way to the rink, somewhere across the glittering green sea, in the farthest reaches of the Arctic, a girl sat up in a cage and hugged her beloved bear.

Siberian sunlight slanted in through the shutters of small wagons built upon sleighs, and The Carnival of Northern Stars, a little band of performers who travelled by husky, darted into the day and began quietly searching for ice.

The carnival which had begun as a small puppet show telling macabre Russian fairy tales had now grown to include a family of acrobats, a Shetland pony who could leap through rings of fire, a fortune teller who supposedly summoned the dead, and a girl and a polar bear who skated hand in paw across the ice with a grace beyond enchantment. *Winter's Promise and Moonrise*

Tuesday.

But it was not an enchantment. It was years and years of discipline and training and unyielding dedication. And though Gretta, who had raised Tuesday and trained Promise, for as long as either of them could remember, choreographed the ice dancing, and supervised training with a heated iron pole, and Yusef who owned the carnival, oversaw every rehearsal with a passion that was unsettling, *really* the entire act, and therefore the fate of the carnival, hung upon the slim shoulders of the girl: Tuesday.

Morning was normally Tuesday's favourite time of day. The sliver of dawn when no one was properly awake and she and Promise—her beloved bear—could roam as they pleased. But this morning they had slept later than usual and after yesterday's appalling rehearsal Tuesday felt uneasy. She wriggled her fingers out of her reindeer hide mitten and reached out to stroke the cold, slender snout that nuzzled her blanketed knees. Two large dark eyes blinked at her with such a tender understanding that she buried her face in his thick downy fur. He smelled of ice-capped mountains and morning dew. 'You're my whole world,' she murmured.

Tuesday said this to Promise every single day, because it was true. And though he couldn't say it back, Tuesday knew in the very core of her bones that he felt it, and showed her with loyalty and the kind of unfaltering love that can only ever come from your family. And that is how they got through season after season in a carnival that owned their freedom. And besides, when they danced together across the ice, Tuesday felt as if nothing else existed but her and her bear and the twilight beyond.

Tuesday took the heavy brass key that hung around her neck and unlocked the cage. Theirs was the only sled-wagon that had no shutters, as if both the girl and the bear needed to sleep in the presence of starlight. How Tuesday stood the cold, nobody really knew; she had many coats and blankets, but really it was the fleecy fur of the bear that protected her. Slipping off a big woollen jacket and pulling on a much sleeker parka she eased her feet into her hand stitched snow boots. 'Come on my Snow Angel,' she said, beckoning the great bear, rubbing her sore wrist as she did so.

Yesterday she and Gretta had had a furious row. It was all because Promise didn't like having his huge skates on all day.

It had always been so. And Gretta had always been ruthlessly strict with him. But as Tuesday got older she felt when her bear was sad, or impatient. She heard the call of the wilderness beyond the carnival when it whispered to him. And she couldn't stand the way Gretta hurt him with the heated iron pole. Yesterday, in the sixth hour of rehearsal, Promise had flailed around impatiently, catching a lock of Tuesday's hair in his claws and nearly dragging her to the ground. But it had been an accident; he was just restless. When Gretta came for him, Tuesday dived between them, her slim wrist raised to deflect the pole.

The pain had made her scream, then Promise had bellowed, Gretta had shrieked in horror and everyone had rushed to help. Once her wrist had been packed with ice, it had taken Tuesday seven minutes to calm her bear down. It normally took under two.

Promise lumbered out of the sled-wagon, his curious jaws already munching on a mouthful of dried bilberries. Running her hand over his soft forehead, Tuesday moved off with a little skip, winding her way amongst the wakening wagons, knowing the great bear was right behind her, plodding in time with her footfall.

There was no snow yet, but the wind was sharp with the presence of ice and the yipping howl of the huskies. *Winter is nigh* thought Tuesday, which was a favourite phrase of Uncle Tolya, the carnival's wizened musician. 'We'll get to dance the new show soon,' Tuesday murmured, feeling a little spark of excitement.

Promise nibbled at the ends of her long corduroy skirt and she pushed his nose away with a gentle boot and a firm 'no.' He gave a small indignant snort and fell back in step with her. It had always been this way. Wherever

Tuesday whirled or wandered, Promise gladly followed. Wherever Promise roamed or rambled, Tuesday raced and rushed behind. They were two wild creatures who moved through the world together.

Girl and Bear. Bear and Girl.

Tilting her chin to the sky, Tuesday went straight to the props sled-wagon. She would get the fire going, as a thank you to her friends and a resented apology to Gretta. The best thing to do after an awful rehearsal was to move on and stay positive.

Like the rest of the carnival, the props wagon was brightly coloured and glorious. Opening the two painted wooden doors at the back, she leaped up into a cramped little room that smelled of moth wings and the end of summer.

She ducked beneath a row of copper pots and retired puppets which were strung from the ceiling, and clambered over a treasure chest of once-splendid costumes. Balancing on her tiptoes she focused her strength, locked her ankles and rose onto point. Poised on the very edge of her straightened toes.

Then, holding her breath, Tuesday wrestled an enormous brass pot down, sank back onto the soles of her feet, gave a little happy sigh, heaved several silver birch logs off the back of the wagon and shoved them inside the pot. She slipped a small, mightily sharp axe into her deep pocket, pushed the pot into the grassy ground and darted out after it, closing the wagon doors and lugging the laden pot into the centre of the wagon pack. The bear sniffed affectionately at her toes. 'No,' said Tuesday, softly pushing his snout away again. Promise gave the littlest growl.

Tuesday turned her full attention to him, staring deep into his wintry eyes. 'Sit,' she said calmly, and he did. 'Hold,' she said a little more sternly, offering him a wide silvered log. Promise clasped the log in his clawed paws, his long eyelashes blinking away a soft falling sleet. Tuesday angled his nose to the side and raised the axe a little way into the air. 'Be still,' she ordered, before bringing the axe down with the smoothness of a woodcutter and splitting the log in half. Two silver moons with dark hearts. *Like Gretta's*, Tuesday thought, a pulse of worry fluttering across her heart.

Ten minutes later a brisk little fire was hissing to life, the crackle of flame drawing the rest of the company out into the pale September day. Tuesday's friend Jude, the Shetland pony handler, gave her a small thankful salute when he saw the fire. And the two weathered puppeteers, Hans and Franco, both winked kindly, while Anushka nodded gratefully, wrangling her half-dressed children into sweaters.

Tuesday at once felt lighter. Things with Gretta were tough, but she loved her strange little carnival and all its odd performers.

A woman in a floor-length wolfskin kimono with a shock of grey hair swept out of her wagon, as if sleep were a thing for the weak of heart. 'Who got the fire going?' she barked, glaring at the fatigued troupe of performers. Tuesday's heart sank into her toes. She should have known better—nothing she ever did pleased Gretta. Not any more. But someone had to get the fire going. After they all rose and searched for ice. It's how they started their day.

Is she still cross with me for yesterday, Tuesday wondered. Lucie, the littlest of the acrobat children tiptoed over to sit beside her, smiling at Promise in quiet awe. Tuesday gave a quick sigh, realizing just why Gretta was seething. Gretta hated it when Promise got too near the other carnival members. It was as if she didn't trust him.

Or she doesn't want me to have any friends, thought Tuesday darkly.

For Tuesday knew Promise would never hurt anyone intentionally. Her skin was glittered with scars that came from the grizzle and gruffness of Promise's teeth, but he'd never bitten her to the bone, never drawn enough blood for a stitch. He could be so tender with the smaller children. Yet still Gretta insisted he remain far from everyone else.

Tuesday hardened her heart and gave a casual flick of her dark and wondrous curls.

'I started the fire,' she answered, gazing directly into the flames.

'It's not your job!' snapped Gretta. The company collectively drew in a breath.

Tuesday stood up. Promise moved in time, looming behind her, his snout resting in her hair. His eyes were the colour of the forest at midnight, his teeth could tear out your throat, and his heart beat only for Tuesday.

Tuesday put her hands on her hips, knowing she was protected. Gretta regarded them both coldly. The other artists fidgeted nervously.

'And if you are going to join us for breakfast,' Gretta half spat, 'leave that beast in the wagon. He's a working animal not a pet.'

Tuesday flinched, a fury beginning to rise in her.

Behind her Promise gave a low, steady growl, soft as breath, but full of power.

Gretta glared at the bear hatefully but said nothing. Then she stalked off to get the oats and the goat, for porridge.

All around her, Tuesday saw people's huddled shoulders relax. But she felt deeply worried.

What if Gretta takes it out on Promise at rehearsal, or withholds his food?

The carnival normally did well for food in the summer months, hunting the small white Arctic animals that weren't as well camouflaged without snow. But during the winter they relied mostly on fish, dried berries, nuts, and milk from the goat. Promise had never learned to hunt for himself, and Yusef was always moaning that he ate too many of their supplies, and didn't pay his way. This angered Tuesday. They didn't get paid at all, so it was impossible for either of them to pay their way.

I'll have to speak to Gretta.

Tuesday beckoned to her friend Jude, who had a natural affinity with animals and was about the only other performer who was confident with the bear. 'Can you watch him for two minutes?' she asked. Jude subtly moved closer to Promise and nodded. 'Stay here boy,' Tuesday said in a low voice that was still full of command, and keeping her beloved bear in her sight lines she wove a winding path after Gretta.

'Tuesday!' Gretta's voice was sharp but not cross; still, it startled Tuesday and she stumbled backwards. 'What are you doing? Trying to sneak up on me?'

Tuesday swallowed. 'I wanted to apologize. For bringing Promise to breakfast,' she lied. Gretta's frown melted away and she gave a tired smile. 'I thought you might like to apologize to me too,' Tuesday added, scrunching her toes up to give herself courage.

To her surprise Gretta gave a low chuckle, pulled a small bucket out of the animal wagon, turned it upside down and settled herself on it, gesturing for Tuesday to sit on the ground close by her.

'I am sorry that you got hurt yesterday. But Tuesday, what you did was dangerous. You understand that you and Promise have to listen to everything I say.'

'I know, but Promise was exhausted and I just wanted to—'

'That's not for you to decide.'

Tuesday turned her face away trying to stop the mounting anger.

Gretta reached out and tucked a tendril of Tuesday's long hair behind her ear. 'On that first night, when Promise brought you home, neither of you would sleep without the other. So I kept you both with me.'

Tuesday sat up taller and turned to face Gretta. She knew this story of course—the tale of her arrival. But Gretta rarely spoke about it anymore.

You came from a land that was wonderful, and your parents loved you very much. But from the moment they laid eyes on you, they knew you were different, special, for you were born with snowflakes glittering in your hair and the mark of a paw upon your heart. So they sought out the one carnival in the world which had an ice bear. They left you on the ice in the middle of the night for Promise to find and bring inside.

Did they say goodbye? Did they leave a note? No need my love, they knew this was your destiny and they were honoured to help you achieve it.

'I wrapped you together in a blanket embroidered with stars. You, with your jewel-bright eyes. And

Promise, with his killer claws. I knew you were destined to be together. Promise found his way to *North Star*. He chose this, and he chose you.'

Tuesday knew Gretta was right, that Promise loved skating as much as she did. That he loved her more than anything else, only she felt his wildness and sometimes she longed to let him roam freely.

'I had never meant to let you both sleep side by side forever,' Gretta continued, a thin thread of regret weaving its way around her words. 'But you were always so wilful, so wayward. And Promise so windswept and winter-hearted. Together you were unstoppable. But I can see now, that was a mistake.'

Tuesday felt herself go still.

'I know you and Promise are the soul of the carnival, but you must listen to me Tuesday, otherwise I'll have to separate you both except for rehearsals. I won't tolerate this insolence any more.'

'I'm sorry, I'm sorry,' cried Tuesday, genuinely meaning it. 'I'll do everything you say, from now on. I—I promise. For Promise.'

'As you should . . . now go and find your bear.'

And Tuesday scuttled away feather-light on her feet, back to the bear that was her family.

'We belong here boy. We belong. So we have to do as Gretta says,' she whispered into his fur.

Two large eyes met hers, serious and deep, and

Tuesday felt a small fissure of worry at the edge of her heart.

Promise doesn't trust Gretta she thought, *and nor do I.*

Chapter 4

THE RINK

Marv gave a swift little grin as he caught sight of the rink. It was built in the hollow of Mount Maplewood and was open all year, so even on the coldest, deepest nights you could see it flickering from anywhere on the island, like a guiding star for lost travellers.

The girls' junior team were busy training and the car park was mostly empty, but for the yellow Arctic poppies which grew up through the flattened grass no matter the season.

Marv stood still breathing in the mist, shivering a little as it froze his cheeks. A shadow moved in his periphery and he went still.

'Looking for a lost baby?' Kobi's voice was brimming with scorn. Marv tried not to react. Tried to calm his thumping heart. He darted a glance at the rink door, knowing that just on the other side of it was Coach.

Maybe he should act as if he had headphones on and move inside. But there wasn't time; Kobi was already rounding on him. 'Thing I don't get Jackson, is how you could possibly fight a bear when you won't even fight another kid?'

This wasn't entirely true—Marv had thrown a smoothie over Kobi once in the ice rink's coffee shop. It hadn't exactly been his finest moment and thankfully Coach stepped in before Kobi could act.

Marv felt his grip tighten on his stick. He locked his knees so they wouldn't tremble, put his skates down, and let his bag slide to the ground. Kobi was only a year older than him, but he was strong from years of rigorous training and Marv barely reached his shoulder. Glancing at him, Marv noticed Kobi's cheek was already smarting with a bruise, probably from hockey. But his t-shirt looked filthy.

'What's it to be Jackson?'

There was nothing else for it. Marv could either run, or take the hit.

'Jackson. Stone. Good to see you both.' A voice like midsummer sunshine warmed the air, and the tension melted like butter. Kobi dropped his stick and Marv pushed his cap back in surprise, both of them grinning at a tall guy with twinkling eyes and a kilowatt smile.

'Florian!' Marv cried, recovering the quickest.

For Florian was the dream. The real thing. A boy

who had won game after game after game until his name was sung so loudly that the wind carried it across the sea, through the tundra and over the mountains to the beachside city of Vancouver and he was offered a place with the Canucks. 'I thought you were in Vancouver? I thought the season was starting?'

Florian gave a little shrug. 'What and miss out coaching you lot. Don't be silly,' he laughed.

'What, you came back from Vancouver just to train us?' asked Kobi, sounding genuinely astonished.

Florian winked at him kindly. 'Yep . . . that, and I might be going to my sister's wedding.'

Marv chuckled and Kobi tried to look sullen without quite managing it. Florian gave the boys a light salute. 'I'll see you up there in five,' he said in that easy way that made you want to smile.

Kobi picked his stick up and stalked away, the fire gone from him. Marv gathered up his skates and stepped into the rink.

It was like stepping into a cloud of spun silver or breathing in lightning. He felt the cold tug at him, nipping at his bones. He hurried through the little coffee bar, past the reception, which only really opened for the tourists in darkest winter, up the stairs, down a draughty corridor full of dust-kissed trophy cabinets and into the locker rooms.

They were still reasonably clean, having been empty

most of the summer. As his teammates got ready around him Marv pulled on all the padding, then perched on a bench and pushed his feet into his skates. He winced slightly as he felt the boot pinch his toes. *I can't have grown out of them already.*

Since Marv was heralded a hockey hero, his family had never had to pay for his kit, as the local sports store offered him sponsorship. If his stick broke, it was replaced without him asking. If the palm of his glove ripped, then a new set would miraculously appear. If the straps of his shoulder pads wore thin, new ones would arrive like a gift. This was no small feat considering that when the store ran out of stock everything had to be ordered through the Sears catalogue.

Most of Marv's teammates played in hand-me-down kit from their brothers and sisters, endlessly winding their sticks in tape to try to prevent them breaking.

This amongst many other things was one of the reasons Kobi disliked Marv so much. Kobi's dad had been a professional player, one of the island's most famed stars, but a fight on the ice and a terrible injury ended his career. He never quite got over it. Kobi had his dad's talent and even more drive. He should have been the one to have the sponsorship, been the adored mascot, lifted in the air when the older boys won.

Marv wiggled his toes and tightened his laces. The skates were pinching hard, but he'd just have to hang on till November 7th his birthday, for new skates.

'On the ice everyone. Grab a puck,' came a deeper voice, rich as mountain rain. It belonged to Coach. No one knew his name, not even the Jacksons who had spent four Christmases with him, and countless evenings in the warmth of his company, both on and off the ice. He was simply called Coach by everyone. At the commanding age of fifty-eight there wasn't much that escaped him.

As the boys filed out onto the mirror-smooth surface, Coach moved seamlessly onto the ice in his beloved beaten-up skates, his voice filling the rink twice over. 'Got a special treat for you all today,' he continued, his face crinkling into a smile, before he melted serenely back to the sides.

'Hey guys!' Florian grinned, gliding onto the ice, arms wide, smile wider. A collective gasp of glee swept through Marv's team and they almost forgot themselves. Almost flocked around him, like cygnets to a swan.

Marv skated over to a small quick boy named Sol Cooper—his best friend. They nodded at each other as Florian laid a set of orange cones in an angled line.

'OK listen up,' he said, giving a single clap that could have silenced the world. 'I'll be your coach today, and if at the end of training you're selected, you'll get the chance to come on tour in November.' This time everyone did gasp. 'You'll play a team from Churchill, then Winnipeg, then you can come and skate on our training rink in Vancouver—maybe meet some of the team.' Now the boys were falling over themselves, a joyful din rising to the rooftop.

'That's so awesome. That's like a week's tour,' breathed Sol.

'Ten days,' Florian mouthed. 'Skate through the cones, fast as you can. Then do the same backwards, keep the puck with you.' There was a small beat of hesitation. It was one thing to move over the ice on blades of steel, stick in hand, bent low so you could race as fast the wind. Skating backwards at speed and with precision was a little harder.

'Jackson, off you go!' Marv shot forward, his stick held low across his body. Leaning easily on one leg, he brought the other foot in sharp doing a quick chassé, before slaloming between the cones, the puck never leaving the curve of his stick. As he reached the last cone he threw his signature move in, a figure skating trick Mya had taught him. He rose onto the tip of his skates like an ice dancer, balanced on the jagged pick of his blades, and ran around the cone, like a little darting mouse before shooting backwards, with perfect control.

Sol gave him a thumbs-up, Florian gave a subtle wink.

'Stone—helmet on. You're next.'

Kobi left his helmet on the bench, tucked a tendril of red hair behind his ear and drifted across the rink with the air of a child in a daydream. Some of the team rolled their eyes. You never knew what this boy was up to.

Something made Marv look up. He wasn't sure what; some long-standing instinct of knowing when he was being watched. He peered subtly into the stands and there, furthest from the rink, he met the cold eyes of Old Stoney. The man who had shot Marv's bear, Kobi's father. It had only been because the man was drunk that the bear had lived, he had shot her crooked.

Marv felt surprised. It was rare for the man to make an appearance at a match, let alone training. He looked angry, and his hair was a terrible unbrushed mess. His cheeks scarlet like two blemishes.

Marv's gaze flitted back to Kobi.

Did he know his father was watching? Is this why he was acting up?

The red-haired boy paused in front of the cones, slowly stooped, gave a long whistle as if assessing the course. Florian folded his arms, stared directly at him.

'I said get your helmet,' began Florian, but Kobi had already taken off, shooting forward with such power his skates sliced the ice into zigzags.

He zipped between the cones, blades screeching, then flew backwards, the puck almost a blur. Marv's mouth hung open.

'He must have been here, like all summer. Or up at Lake Rarity,' whispered Sol.

Marv nodded, feeling a sudden jab of worry at the thought of Kobi skating in his favourite place. The islands-spectacular mountain top lake.

Kobi flew around the last cone in such a blaze that the heel of his skate knocked it and he tripped, crashing backwards but somehow tucking his knees, turning it into a roll, springing up unscathed. He made a big show of mock wiping sweat from his brow. A cheer of laughter erupted from the team.

Florian did not smile. 'Off the ice, Stone. If you haven't learnt how to put your kit on, you don't get to train with the A team—' Florian began, but Coach cut him off.

'Who thinks this is funny?' The rink fell still. Coach stepped back onto the ice, slippers on his feet, but he still moved with the agility of a skater. Marv darted a glance at Sol. They both knew what was coming.

'Stone, is this a joke to you?' Collectively the team lowered their gaze.

Kobi shook his head in earnest. 'Then don't behave like a clown! Where's your helmet?' Kobi said nothing but pointed to the bench. Coach lent over him; in skates Kobi wasn't far off eye level, yet still Coach seemed to tower over him. 'I catch you in the wrong kit and you'll be suspended from the team.' Kobi's cheeks flushed as red as his hair, he nodded, skated to the bench and eased his helmet on ready to train.

A shadow moved at the back of the stands. Marv squinted into the gloom and saw Old Stoney leaving the rink. He felt an unexpected beat of sympathy for Kobi, humiliated in front of the father he was always trying to impress.

Coach addressed them all now, his voice low but still booming. 'You know what it takes to be a great player?' The boys nodded at him, young eyes bright with the dreams of their futures. 'You got to race, you got to dive, you got to shriek to a halt like you're frozen in time.'

Coach took them all in, his gaze boring through the metal cages and into each boy's heart. 'And you've got to have the right damn kit!' He strode off the ice, and without missing a beat Florian picked up the session.

Marv half hoped Kobi wouldn't make the team. And yet he knew they needed him. If Marv had never been attacked, never got his moon-mark scar, never become Marvel, maybe hockey wouldn't have been so important to him. It was a way for him to exist beyond the story that haunted him. A way for him to be talented for who he was, not because of what had happened to him. Sure the sponsorship, and free coaching, and being made team mascot definitely helped. But the hours of practice in mind-numbing cold, the fearless way he zipped around the ice, a shooting star on skates, the way he controlled the puck with the simplest flick of his wrist . . . all of that came from Marv. From an unyielding will to win.

Training ended and Marv's team flopped onto the rink seats of the auditorium, sweat spilling into their eyes, hearts racing as they caught their breath.

Florian gave them a serious frown before his face broke into a wide grin. 'Guess what?' No one dared guess. 'You're all coming to Vancouver!' A cheer of manic elation echoed round the rink.

It was still singing through Marv's mind when he and Sol stepped outside, a light sleet falling from the sky.

It wasn't quite snow, but *soon*, soon it would be, and Marv couldn't wait. He headed home, through the busy little town of Bearsville and over the River Raven, which already had a thin film of ice at its edges.

And without meaning to, he pictured it frozen, a basket in the middle, a little cub scampering joyfully toward it.

Chapter 5

NORTH STAR

Tuesday slipped her gloves off and pulled hard on the laces of her practice skates, a flutter of excitement gracing her heart as she thought of the ice. The rushing freedom, the breeze in her hair, the speed that let her leap as high as Promise's shoulders.

I just want to skate and skate and skate forever.

The air was laced with October mist and it wouldn't be long until the sea froze over and the carnival set off on their winter adventure.

Tuesday's practice skates were made from faded brown leather, bound together with old cord, which frayed a little more every time she fastened them. But they had to be tight. It was almost impossible to leap with a loose skate, or balance on a jagged-edged pick. And Tuesday couldn't risk an injury. She had to have command of her edges.

The blades themselves, like Promise's, were carved from bone. Just like the very first skates ever worn by early ice-dwellers, Gretta had fashioned them herself, hardly changing the design. It was a lot cheaper than paying the postage for skates to be shipped to whichever far-flung outpost town they were staying near. And no one anywhere would make boots to fit a bear. So Gretta had got Hans and Franco, the puppet-makers, *to* craft a solid open-toed sole, like a rock-hard sandal fitted with blades, that could be bound to Promise's foot, leaving his paws free to wiggle.

It wasn't even a dress rehearsal, but still Yusef treated every moment upon the ice as if time were a currency as rare as diamonds, and if anyone got anything wrong his mood could become unbearable.

'Foot,' she said, gently holding out his enormous flat-soled skate. Promise gave a sleepy grunt, wiggled onto his back, and with the gentleness of a dancer held out his paw. Tuesday slipped the soft leather binding over his foot. His skates were much wider than figure skater's, and instead of one blade for Promise to balance his colossal weight on there were two, so each skate was like a miniature sleigh. In place of laces or ribbon, there was rope.

Tuesday bound his skates as firmly as she could, then squeezed her fingers between the top of the skate and Promise's furry leg, making sure there was enough space for him to bend his knees. His leg felt so thin beneath her hands.

She pushed her long matted curls out of her eyes and tried not to chew her lip. Tuesday didn't know any other bears. She had seen them at a distance, out patrolling the ice, but up close she wasn't sure how they were meant to look. *Maybe not this thin* she thought, a cold claw of fear scratching at her heart. 'I'll get you more food. We'll go out tonight and find berries, or a rabbit or a baby bird, a whole feast just for you.'

Promise grunted and pushed his snout into Tuesday's wild curls, absentmindedly munching on one. Her hair was almost black, but on the nights Anushka helped her brush oil through her curls and the moonlight fell across it, you could see it was streaked with indigo.

'Come on my darling,' Tuesday whispered, tugging Promise gently onto all fours, then standing in front of him, and slowly turning away so her back was to her bear. 'Rise,' she said, and snapped her fingers.

With a little stagger Promise rose onto his back feet, balancing for moment on his blades before leaning his front paws upon Tuesday's young shoulders—claws and all. Tuesday hardly noticed. It was hard for Promise to walk on land in the skates, but they took so long to fasten properly, Yusef would have an absolute fit if Promise arrived at rehearsals without the right kit on. So this was the only way they could get there, a small girl balancing a bear.

The rest of *North Star*—as it was affectionately called by its performers—were gathered around a small makeshift stage, marked out along the edge of a river. There was Uncle Tolya, solemnly playing his ancient accordion. Bright-eyed, serious Jude, clasping the rains of Bressay his fire-jumping Shetland pony. Hans and Franco the puppet-makers, who stayed up so late that they themselves had begun to look as if they were held together by thread. Anushka and Sebastian the chief acrobats, and their four tumbling children. All of them gazing at Tuesday with a soft sense of awe.

In the middle of the river a single stray iceberg had become wedged between two rocks, creating a little platform. This was the best they could do for a rink. Zarina the fortune teller was sailing across it, dramatically throwing her arms out as if casting hot coals from her fingers, yelling 'Spirits . . . spirits of the forest, show me your souls, tell me your story.'

Tuesday wanted to give her a little cheer. Her commitment to the role of spirit summoner was so vivid, it was mesmerizing.

I hope we get big audiences this winter, Tuesday thought. *I hope the whole of Canada comes to the carnival.*

After two seasons in Russia and Greenland with a scattering of people turning up to each show, and the takings of the carnival becoming smaller and smaller,

Gretta and Yusef needed to seek out bigger crowds. 'Not everyone wants to see a dancing bear,' Jude had told Tuesday in confidence. 'Some people are against it. That's why we move about so much, always sticking to the ice or Tundra. So the authorities can't catch up with us.'

Tuesday ran her eyes over the little iceberg, checking for dips or bumps and cracks that might trip them up; thankfully, it looked quite smooth. She gave a small grateful nod to Franco and Hans, knowing it was one of them who would have chiselled the ice down, after Gretta had no doubt spent half the night searching it out.

'Ready Tuesday!' came Yusef's sharp voice from across the bank. No matter the season, Yusef always dressed as if he were an artist in Paris. A dark blue beret, a mustard neckerchief, a paisley shirt of some nature, ankle-length jeans, and shoes you might wear in a library. The only alteration he made for the snow was to add an elaborately thick rabbit skin jacket and snow boots. He didn't even grow a beard.

There was a whiney ring to his voice, so even when he was trying to assert his authority he sounded like a fussy child. Tuesday answered by nodding, placing her bare hands upon Promise's paws, and moving across the uneven grass with a perfectly straight back, her expression focused, her eyes watching closely.

Zarina had finished summoning her ghosts, and now the 'spirits', the family of acrobats, cartwheeled beautifully across the iceberg, arms and legs spinning so fast they looked like dancing stars. Uncle Tolya squeaked and sighed a few sombre notes on the accordion and the carnival held its breath.

Tuesday slipped out of Promise's grip as Jude stepped in to steady the bear's great weight. He gave her a sharp encouraging wink. Tuesday whipped off her blade guards, knelt to do the same for Promise, climbed onto the iceberg, and even though it was just a rehearsal she got that rush, that wave of excitement that washed over her skin and suddenly she was alive.

She flashed Jude a gleaming grin, and thrust out a hand to Promise, easing him onto the ice, one bladed paw at a time. Then Tuesday was glowing from the tips of her sharpened skates to the ends of her wind-whipped curls.

For there was nothing quite like that first moment when she stepped from land to ice, the way her foot slid where seconds before it was still. The way her heart caught in her chest and her bones found balance. The way everything seemed brightly possible, like a dream of flying become real.

She gripped Promise's scarred paws, and gazed into his large trusting eyes. 'I love you,' Tuesday mouthed, and Promise gave a subtle nod as if to say *I know*.

arabesque.

As he careened toward edge of the berg, white paws flailing, his eyes wide with fear, Tuesday shot in front and whipped around to face him. She lurched into Promise, her feet driving into the ice as she landed in a low lunge, wrapping her arms tightly around his middle. His weight hit her chest inching her backwards. Tuesday closed her eyes, gritted her teeth and dug the edge of her blades deep into the ice, so they came to a dramatic stop.

Promise gave a terrified grunt, his claws swiping at Tuesday's poised back as he struggled to catch his balance. Sweat ran into Tuesday's eyes as she forced her legs to hold—at the edge of her vision she saw Gretta approach with the pole, and she clung to her bear willing him to be calm. Slowly, slowly Promise stood still. The company of *North Star* all gave a small tight sigh. Tuesday could have collapsed with relief. She could have sworn or demanded a break or laughed like a nightingale. But she was performer and when she raised her beautiful face it was clear of emotion, her eyes still bright with doll-like wonder, her nimble body ready to finish the act.

By the end of the routine everyone was applauding and smiling once again. Yusef didn't seem to mind the melodramatic mid-scene rescue. *He'll probably make it part of the act* thought Tuesday grimly. From between the trees Gretta flashed her a tight-lipped scowl, but she didn't say anything. Tuesday's poor heart was hammering.

She helped her beloved bear off the ice and sat down on a mossy tree stump to ease his skates off. Promise's expression was blank, his breathing heavy. *Is he dizzy? Is he tired? Is he hungry?* Tuesday wondered, mopping his damp furry brow and checking his blades.

She hissed a small curse. One of the four blades was blunter than normal. Skaters' blades should have a slight curve to them like a slither of moonlight. The less curved they are the harder it is to use your edges. Without sharp edges you are lost upon the ice. Tuesday quietly dropped the skate and put her head in her hands, hot tears falling from her eyes.

'It's my fault,' she sighed, between gulps. *It could have all gone so wrong, all because of a blunt skate. Promise might have fallen. Might have got hurt—or Gretta would have blamed him and got the dreaded pole.*

As Tuesday quietly wept, Promise gave a sad sigh, rolled onto his four feet, and began softly butting Tuesday's trembling shoulders. She leant her head on his warm cheek, his wet nose nuzzling her neck. 'Alright boy,' she said after a moment, 'let's get you some food.' And the girl and the bear set off together into the forest, searching for berries and nuts, their young hearts beating to the very same rhythm.

Chapter 6

HALLOWEEN

Marv perched on the edge of the couch, reluctantly adjusting an old American trucker's cap, which Leon had fixed a real pair of stag antlers to. Indi had sprayed them silver and Mya had draped them with cobwebs, in keeping with this year's theme of woodland animals. The antlers looked both creepy and ethereally marvellous. But Marv found them kind of heavy.

It was hard for him to really concentrate on anything else, when the bears were this close. It was as if he'd grown so in tune with the island that he knew the very moment a bear set foot on land. And it tugged at his bones with a subtle certainty. And always the glittering hope that soon he would see *his bear* outshine everything else.

'Is that it for your costume?' demanded Mya. She was dressed as a rather superb hipster-squirrel. Her face was painted lipstick red and two felt ears she'd attached to a headband popped out from her bunched hair. A huge bushy tail, created from a feather duster and coat hanger wire, was pinned to top of her orange ski leggings.

Marv suddenly wondered if he should have made more effort, but he hated dressing up.

He high-fived Mya—she looked kind of bonkers but cool. Then he raised the brim of his cap and saw Rae—Trucker's daughter—lingering behind Mya on the stairs.

She was draped in a long white dress of Indi's, adorned with soft feathers. Mya had fastened a sheet to the back of it and tied the corners around Rae's wrists so when she raised her arms she had makeshift wings. Mya had fixed a tiny paper beak over Rae's nose. When she stepped into the kitchen and did a slow spin, the effect was quite mesmerizing.

'You're an owl.' Marv half smiled. The front door flew open and Leon stepped inside, brushing fresh snow from his jacket.

'Come and look at your brilliant children, Mr Jackson. See how fierce they look,' Indi said.

Leon peered round the kitchen. If he was tired after a long shift at the island's tiny airport, he didn't show it. 'You guys look great.' He wiped frost from his eyebrows and pulled on an antler cap that matched Marv's but was slightly bigger and made him look very majestic.

Leon was the air traffic controller, and the keeper of keys for the airport. Mostly his job was managing flights around the weather, making sure people came and went from the island safely, something which was mighty tricky in the winter.

'Ready to go?' Leon opened the front door.

Marv felt a jitter of excitement—or was it nerves—take hold of him. Would the bears come tonight? He felt sure that they would.

Outside the street was already filling up with families traipsing through the snow toward town, all brandishing fire. During the winter, islanders never went out alone after dark. They drove in groups if the roads were clear enough, or they travelled in little gangs skating along the River Raven or tramping through the busier streets bearing lit torches. There was something fiercely wonderful about carrying flames.

Indi fixed a garland of Ivy to her hair and flung a long moss green cloak over her clothes. It made her look like the goddess of the winter woods. 'Ready guys,' she called, sweeping out of the door and gazing back at the gang of woodland children. Just for a moment, Marv saw the woman Indi might have been without the bear attack. Someone lighter on her feet, someone who could glide through the world unhindered, someone who never surrendered to fear.

Everyone tumbled and clambered out into skittering

snowfall, giggling and squealing with delight as Leon handed them each a huge lit branch. Sleet sparkled and spat in the firelight and the sky looked dark and delightful; the whole island seeming to burn with strange magic.

As they reached the bottom of the hill, a sudden shrill whisper swirled through the crowds. Marv felt prickles roll over his skin, his bones trembling a little with both fear and hope. *Is it her? Had she come to the island early?*

Mya turned back to her brother, her hazel eyes shining through her squirrel make-up. 'A bear,' she mouthed, and Marv's heart softly fluttered. *My bear?* He closed his eyes for a moment and felt through the dark night air, but couldn't feel anything beyond the excitement of the crowd.

Everyone hurried on in a nervous silence, joining the group of fire-bearing folk who had congregated at the bottom of the hill. Indi glanced anxiously at her son, and without speaking, Leon reached out and took his wife's hand. A stillness fell across everyone so the only sound was the crackle of the fire and stolen gasps of breath.

Then a little girl somewhere in the crowd called out 'Look Mommy—a bear. An ice bear.' And the crowd turned their head as one, gazing along the path that led to the sea. For there, padding on lethal paws came a giant, regal as a king. Snout down, sniffing the ground, sharp eyes searching. Beneath his silver antlers the boy with a moon-mark scar began to shimmer.

A bear! Though as the beautiful beast drew closer Marv could see it was not his bear. She would not come early this year. He gave a short rushing sigh, and Sol who had found him in the crowd, gave him a little frown and a swift thumbs-up—like they did on the ice. Marv gave a thumbs-up back, signalling he was fine.

He wasn't sure quite what he felt. The return of his bear made the strange memory of the baby seem more real. As if the bear somehow knew that there had been a babe and a cub that night on the frozen river, and she was there to make sure Marv never forgot.

I will never forget though. I've got the scar he thought with an almost grin. And he slipped his fingers free of his glove and reached up to touch his cheek.

Around Marv the folk of the Isle of Bears were still enthralled by the creature for which they were named. But as the bear lifted its solemn head, dark eyes gleaming with feral intent, the townsfolk melted back up the various hilly streets toward their homes. The Polar Patrol officers were alerted to come and keep an eye on the bear, and Halloween for now was to continue inside, with everyone feasting on sweets they'd been given by their neighbours.

Soon the Jacksons' kitchen was steamy with the smell of bubbling hot chocolate, music was playing, Indi and

Leon were dancing together in the kitchen, while Marv, Mya, and their friends were piled on the stairs. Sol had joined them, bringing a big slice of his mom's apple and pumpkin-seed cake. He was sitting next to Rae as they all shared it.

'That was definitely Fraser,' said Sol, referring to the bear.

'How can you tell?' scoffed Rae.

'From the way he walks,' explained Sol. 'He always travels alone and he always goes straight to town to ransack bins.'

Fraser was a real old troublemaker. Marv was secretly very fond of him; Fraser couldn't really help it, he just loved meat more than fish.

'I don't know how you can tell them apart,' sighed Mya. 'They all look the same apart from—well—your bear,' she said, smiling at her brother.

'I'd love to see that bear up close,' added Sol dreamily.

'Yeah, then I guess you'd have to fight her and end up with a scar like Marv did,' Mya boasted, her face aglow with pride.

'Mya that's not—' Marv began, but Sol cut him off.

'She's right—it's kind of amazing what happened to you, Marv. Honestly, like no other kids on the whole island, probably the entire world, have ever been that close to an actual ice bear.'

Rae raised her owl mask. 'My mama said there's this

circus in Greenland who have a girl that skates with a bear.'

Mya opened her eyes wide with amazement. 'A polar bear?'

Rae nodded. 'Mama's never seen it, but she heard about it when she went home to look after my grandmother.'

'A girl who dances with a bear?' said Marv slowly, his spine beginning to tingle. *Just like in my dream.*

Rae nodded.

'That's impossible,' laughed Sol, but beneath the paper beak of her owl mask, they could all see that Rae was serious.

'I guess it could be possible,' said Marv, trying to work it out, 'if, like, the girl was an awesome animal tamer or something.'

Rae, who had grown up around nature, living off the land as the woods-folk did, shook her head. 'No,' she said gently. 'My Dad has raised all kind of wild animals. He's always lived in the forest. If the girl and bear had grown up together, they'd have a special respect for each other. That's the only way it could work.'

There was a silence that held many unspoken questions and Rae suddenly became self-conscious beneath the weight of it. 'I mean you know—either that or she's some millionaire princess who has thousands of exotic pets and dances with them for fun . . .' Her voice trailed off and at that moment a car horn sounded outside.

Indi appeared with Rae's coat. 'Sweetheart, that's your dad outside.' Everyone flocked to the window to wave goodbye as Rae climbed daintily into her Dad's truck. There were few folk who would drive in snow this thick, especially uphill. But being an ice road trucker, who was named after his skills, Trucker didn't find it a problem.

Marv wished Rae could have stayed all night, wished he could have asked her more questions about this weird circus, wished he could have known more about the girl who danced with a bear. And later that night, when everyone was asleep he found himself going over her words in his mind.

If the girl and the bear had grown up together they'd have a mutual respect for each other.

And he fell to sleep with those words going over and over in his head.

Hours later, Marv sat up in bed, drenched in sweat. He kicked off the duvet and moved to the window, peering out at the windswept island. Sleek white snow coated everything, looking eerie and otherworldly in the lingering winter's moonlight.

He shook his head, trying to shake fragments of the frosted dream away, knowing it would do no good. It was the same dream he often had. The dream of the girl and the bear. It was both beautiful and harrowing.

In the dream Marv was always lost, out on the icy sea, or skating through a blizzard on a lake he didn't know, searching for her. He was never entirely certain who *she* was, but Marv supposed she was the baby from the River Raven—grown into a child.

There would always come a moment in the dream when Marv thought it too cold to go on. Just as he was about to give up, he would see her, far on the horizon, dancing beneath a sweeping night sky. The storm would still, and the girl would see him. Look at him, across the ice and the years and the falling snow. Then she would fly toward him, arms outstretched, and Marv would bend low and race to meet her, ignoring the pain in his ankles. But they never found each other.

Sometimes the heart-wrenching roar of the mama bear would split the sky and ice in two, and Marv and the girl would both be trapped on two separate sides. Other times, an endless shadow would fall across Marv, blotting out the moon and coating the world in the thickest dark so he would lose sight of the girl completely. Or other times, a gloriously graceful white bear would prance beneath the northern stars, and the girl would forget Marv altogether, curling away from him as she swept after the young bear.

Marv peered through the misted glass. So often when he was younger he had woken in the night in a fit of terror, believing the baby was still out there. On those nights, Indi would sit with him for hours stroking his hair. 'It's possible there was a baby,' she had eventually agreed, as throughout the history of the island there had been other children rescued from the ice. Those children ended up being the stuff of legends who were sung about in ballads and lullabies. Babies who fell mistakenly off the back of a sleigh. Babies whose parents died protecting them from the winter. Babies who were left as gifts, like the strange Nevkian fairy tale about *The Ice Daughter.*

These were the gentle stories Indi whispered to her son, and often to Mya who woke up and crept into bed with them both until Leon got home at four in the morning.

And though Marv felt reassured to know his family believed him, it did nothing to answer the question that burnt like a rare blue flame in his soul.

Where did the baby go?

No one could really answer this. The Jacksons all supposed that a travelling community had saved her from the bear. But Marv wasn't so sure. Until now.

Now he found himself thinking about the circus Rae had mentioned, with the ice dancing girl and her polar bear, and the small blue flame in his heart began to burn a little brighter.

A week later, on the morning of his birthday, Marv awoke to a sky grey as the wing of a gull and clouds heavy with the promise of more snow. He felt the strange jolt he got in his chest every year, waiting and wondering if his bear would come. He'd been waiting all week and now the day was here, anticipation making him giddy.

'Hey, birthday boy!' cried Mya thumping on the door. 'You'll never guess what Mom and Dad have got you!'

Marv smiled, hurrying downstairs still in his pyjamas.

The box was wrapped in navy tissue paper and tiny silver stars.

'These ones are different son,' grinned Leon. 'I got Florian to send them from the skate shop he uses in Vancouver.' Marv moved across the room and hugged him. That would have cost an absolute fortune. He kissed Indi who was rosy-cheeked from her morning swim. She sipped a coffee, watching her son as he carefully unfolded the paper, handing it back to her to be recycled next year, then did a genuine gasp of surprise.

They were different. Black and smooth as glass with cherry-red laces and thick blades of steel. 'Boots made for battle,' Leon chuckled, pulling Marv's cap off over his eyes.

Marv's heart did a small flip. *I can't wait to try them.* Of course he'd have to break them in, let his ankles work their way into the leather, maybe leave them on the radiator or get Indi to pop them in the oven to soften them up a little. But there was nothing quite like the wonder of new skates.

'This is from me. You'll hate it, but you'll thank me one day,' Mya explained, handing him a present that could only be a book.

Marv wrinkled his face into a squint. 'Cheers sis,' he mumbled, reluctantly opening it. Then Marv stared at it in surprise. It was a book of Nevkian myths: *The Ice Daughter and Other Stories*. Beautifully illustrated in every colour of winter. Marv had seen it in the school library, and Sol's family had a French copy at home, but he'd never imagined owning the book himself. It was like holding a piece of a frozen treasure.

He slipped it into the bookcase thanking his sister but vaguely wondering if he would ever actually read it.

The day seemed to pass in a few joyful frozen breaths. Marv left his skates on at the end of training. It was six thirty and the streets were still busy with cars and trucks. There was a small group of hockey players who could skate home along the River Raven, torches held high like shields, helmets on, bodies bent into the wind. And the speed they travelled at, despite it being up hill was easily twenty-five miles an hour.

All the while Marv kept glancing left to right, studying the snow-covered streets, whipping round on razor-sharp blades and shooting backwards, surveying the landscape, searching for her. His bear.

Indi and Mya were waiting for Marv in the lounge. Indi had made hot chocolate and Mya had lit tiny star-shaped candles that emitted a soft gold glow. The room smelled of snow and pine needles and the faint hint of heartbreak.

It was a strange birthday ritual. A ritual that marked the return of the very creature that almost ended his life. It should have been terrifying, but it was not.

Traipsing ice into the house, Marv took his helmet off and sat down on the sofa. It was a different leather sofa to the one he'd slept on eight years ago, but it was in the same place. His mum and sister sat either side of him, each taking hold of one of his gloved hands, and there the boy with the moon-mark scar waited for his birthday visitor.

Time ticked by, but the Jacksons hardly moved. Leon got home from work early and quietly joined them.

They heard her before they saw her. A soft soulful growling, like an injured animal. A bear who had once been struck by a silver bullet. Ever so softly the Jacksons moved to the window. Outside in the street the snowfall had stilled and the wind seemed to be resting. In the middle of the road, directly outside Marv's weather-beaten house was a mother bear as motionless as the waning moon.

If ever you are lucky enough to see an ice bear up close, you will know they have a beauty that can draw tears, even from those with the hardest of hearts. They are exquisite in the grace of their own deadly potential. Hunters of the highest order, cut from claw and cloud. But in the same breath they are spellbindingly lovely.

Even Indi was moved by the bear's majesty. The very first year the bear had turned up, after the attack, Leon had called Polar Patrol, who had shepherded the bear away with trucks and loaded stun guns. But year after year she returned in peace, to the place of the attack by the River Raven, never threatening them, just sombrely gazing at Marv. With time the family just let her come.

As Marv looked into the eyes of the bear, he felt as if he were staring across all of time, into a soul as knowing as the night, who murmured questions borne of the same mystery. *Where are the cub and the girl?*

'Mom,' said Marv softly, steeling his courage, 'Rae mentioned this carnival who have a bear and a girl who skate together.' Mya nodded her support beside him. But the look Indi gave him was so spectacularly sad that it made Marv wish he could snatch the words back. 'Sounds ridiculous right,' he said, forcing a smile as Indi reached out and stroked his scar.

'We've been through this before, honey. Maybe there was a baby, and I'm sure there was a cub, and maybe they are out there somewhere, somehow, we just won't ever know.'

Marv nodded in agreement. Though he did not agree at all.

I do know. They're out there. And I know.

'You've got a big day tomorrow. Better get some sleep,' said Leon. Marv nodded and headed upstairs to take his kit off and pack it up for the epic hockey tour they were setting off on tomorrow. Seeing Florian always lifted Marv's spirits; the two of them had been buddies ever since Marv was made team mascot, when he'd been small enough to sit on Florian's shoulders.

The bear gave a long, low, soulful growl and Marv gazed at her sadly, and turned away from the window, feeling a light tug at his heart as he did so.

But Marv was not the only one to hear the sorrowful wail of the bear, for the wind was full of mischief that night. Every so often it swirled up in little sparkling tempests that snatched at the snow and stole the lonely cry of the howl, carrying it away over the edges of the snow-swept island, across the ice sheets which once were sea, to a carnival that travelled by husky which was racing the stars across the vast northern sky.

Chapter 7

THE STARLIT REHEARSAL

In the cage that was their wagon Promise sat up, his ears flattened by the roar of the wind, deep eyes open wide in alarm. He gave a low disgruntled snort. 'What is it boy?' soothed Tuesday, leaning over and stroking his snow-coloured snout. He licked her hand but a lost look flitted across his eyes. Tuesday leaned closer to him listening hard and she thought she caught the echoing call of another bear.

Tuesday loved it when they travelled by night. Apart from performing this was her favourite thing about life in the carnival. The panting joy of the dogs, the way the wagons felt like they were flying, the moon beaming down from her starry perch.

Since the snowfall, and the sea freezing, Gretta had been in a much merrier mood. Rehearsals had been a joy. For no matter how much Tuesday sometimes loathed

Gretta, she could not deny what an incredible coach the brittle old woman was, pushing Tuesday and Promise to accomplish absolute miracles upon the ice.

'It's an eyelash moon tonight,' Tuesday giggled, wrapping her arms around her bear. He pushed his nose into a little gap between the bars and gave a soft mournful yelp. Tuesday tried to follow his gaze but they were moving too fast and the only constant landmark was the moon.

Jude was at the front guiding the dogs for their wagon, its sleigh-like runners glancing off the ice at such speed they left a trail of sparks in their wake. Theirs was always the last of the wagons—the heaviest because it carried the carnival's star attraction: *Winter's Promise and Moonrise Tuesday.*

There came a shrill below of *'HALT'* from somewhere up ahead and Jude began to slow the wagon. Tuesday peered out across the frozen sea. The ice was black as the night sky and speckled with silver. Beyond the reflection of the eyelash moon far to her right she saw the glimmer of electric light. *What is that?* she wondered, peering hard at the dark shape upon which the lights seemed to twinkle.

'It looks like land,' she murmured, 'like a big rock in the middle of the sea. An island?' It was more than possible, there were so many little islets and glacial communities in the Arctic. Tuesday had just never seen this one, so close to Canada and seemingly alive with people.

She waited till the wagon finally glided to a smooth stop then took the key from her pocket, unlocked the cage, and slipped out onto the silken ice, closing the cage behind her. 'Wait here boy,' she beamed, blowing a sullen-looking Promise a kiss through the bars. Tuesday was wearing her snow boots, but she moved with the easy grace of a skater, gliding around to the front of the wagon and hopping up beside Jude.

His eyes were streaming and his cheeks were rosy red and caked with ice. 'Is that an Island?' she asked, pointing a mittened hand. Jude shielded his brow and stared hard.

'Not sure.' He frowned. 'But I can try and find out when the show opens.' Tuesday gave him a sparkling grin. *The new show!*

This was the thing *North Star* had been working hard for all summer: the new show. It was called *The Enchanted Toyshop* and opened in five days. They had two more days of travel, then three full-on days of rehearsal, before opening night just off the coast of a wind-beaten, snow-kissed town called Churchill.

'I can't wait for the SHOW!!!' Tuesday cried in a rush, almost hugging Jude. He flicked his hair out of his eyes and suppressed a grin.

Yusef leapt down from the front of his sled-wagon,

buttoned his rabbit skin jacket, straightened his cravat, and fetched the saw and hammer from the prop wagon. Tuesday turned to Jude and rolled her eyes as they watched Yusef hand the equipment to Uncle Tolya, Hans, and Franco supervising as the older men cut and smashed a small circular hole in the ice.

Gretta emerged in her wolfskin kimono, her face alarmingly happy. *She loves night travel as much me,* Tuesday realized. For when the freezing wind burnt her skin with its brightness, and the starlight seemed so fresh she could almost taste it, and the wolf-like cry of the huskies sang to her heart, the raw joy of living on the ice felt like magic.

Soon a fire was roaring. Sebastian, Jude, and some of the acrobat children were fishing for supper. Uncle Tolya was bubbling a big pot of borscht, and Zarina was stewing a bright red fruit wine, which smelled so pungent it sent Tuesday reeling backwards.

Hans and Franco sat on a pile of rugs around the fire trying out different voices for a small family of mice puppets they'd made. Lucie danced around them laughing, while Anushka peeled potatoes, quietly watching.

Tuesday moved around the edge of the group, walking a ring around her world. Her carnival, her family. The chickens quietly clucked in their wagons, the dogs sat calm and contented after their long run, occupied with chewing bones. Bressay gave a quiet whinny as Tuesday stroked her dark mane.

'Come and get some supper love,' called Gretta cheerily. Tuesday gave a welcome nod and took a step forward, then her heart caught on something and she felt eyes the colour of the forest at midnight gleaming at her. She peered at Promise's sad quiet face, and as softly as a dove taking flight, Tuesday glided over the ice and kissed his snout through the bars of the cage. The smell of borscht and berry wine drifted by on the breeze. Promise flared his nostrils.

He's hungry . . . And he's been in the wagon all day.

The key felt heavy in Tuesday's pocket, her palm was sweating inside her mitten and her heart was drumming against her bones as she took a long breath, scrunched up her toes, and unlocked the cage.

Promise gave her a quick bewildered glance before he all but tumbled out of it, shaking his head in the moonlight. Reaching up, Tuesday laid a steady hand on the back of his neck. 'Follow,' she said with a clear command, then turned and walked toward the fire, a bear-like shadow moving in step with her. The *Carnival of Northern Stars* fell silent as the girl and the bear arrived in the glow of firelight. It was rare for Promise to be out of his cage at night. And almost unheard of for Tuesday to bring him to supper.

He needs to feel the ice as much as I do, Tuesday reasoned

to herself. Though really she just couldn't stand leaving her beloved bear alone in his cage.

Anushka stiffened a little at the nearness of the bear, but when she saw Lucie look at Promise with a sense of wonder she relaxed. Yusef said nothing but gave an anxious frown; the rest of *North Star* all greeted her with soft encouraging smiles.

Without speaking Uncle Tolya handed her two bowls of borscht, not one. Tuesday began to settle herself on the pile of rugs. 'Love . . . where are your manners?' came Gretta's voice, light and precise as crystal. But Tuesday sensed the warning in it and held her breath. 'You can't bring a beast to the dinner table,' Gretta chuckled, though her eyes, when she glared at Tuesday were like lead. Nobody spoke but the world tensed. 'Go on off back to your wagon. Silly child.'

There was a second of stillness, where Tuesday didn't move, and *North Star* gritted their teeth, willing her to stay but knowing she couldn't.

Then the spell was broken and Tuesday stood up, gathered all the hurt into her heart, snuck the two bowls of borscht inside her coat and span with a wondrous grace on her balls of her feet. 'Come boy,' she said, her voice only slightly wavering as she led Promise back to their wagon.

Tuesday locked the cage door behind them, biting down on a tendril of hair to stop herself crying. She hated it when Gretta called Promise a beast. She took a long swig of night air, and settled her bowl upon Promise's haunches like a small furry table. Then the distant dazzle of electric light caught her eye again and she found herself gazing at the mysterious island in the frozen sea. *Who lives there? Could we run there? Could I hide a bear beneath those trees?* She passed Promise his bowl of borscht, laughing as he gobbled it up, the fur around his mouth turning violet.

It was a thought she had often. A secret wish to be free of Gretta. Free of the carnival. Free to run through the wilderness together. But although Tuesday could forage, and craft buttons out of fallen acorns, or stitch a wonderful hat from fur, she couldn't hunt—and neither could Promise. Nor could Tuesday read maps or a compass. So they stayed and danced and got through it together, with love and ice and moonlight.

Yet every winter, Tuesday became more aware of the way people gazed at her in awe, and at her beautiful bear in fear. And a sharp sense of worry pulsed through her blood. What would happen if someone took Promise away from the carnival—sent him to a zoo? Would she be able to live with him . . . ? Probably not. Or what might happen if Gretta got fed up of him, found a new bear or a new act.

Impossible she reckoned, knowing that she and Promise were the very reason people came tramping out of their warm homes on midwinter nights to visit a mysterious carnival.

What would happen if Promise tired of Gretta? Got fed up of the terrible heated pole. Tuesday fidgeted trying to push the thought away, but it grew into a little thorn, spiking her mind with unease.

She took a big gulp of borscht, swallowing it down with all of her doubts. Then tiredness took over and Tuesday pulled up her hood and snuggled down between Promise's front legs to sleep, her dreams flighty and full of moonlit escapes.

The next evening in the gloom of winter dark, *The Carnival of Northern Stars* arrived at an unmarked location, just off the coast of Churchill and at once began setting up for their final dress rehearsal. As Tuesday helped Promise wiggle into his costume, she peered at the set with a quiet sense of wonder.

A rink had been marked on the sea ice, its surface painted black. Two huge oil lamps powered by a small generator were burning brightly, lighting the stage.

Performers were getting set for the opening scene of *The Enchanted Toyshop:* Hans and Franco were carefully arranging a miniature toy box centre stage; a wonderful doll version of Tuesday and Promise were balanced neatly on top of it.

The acrobat family were already dressed as 'Spirits of the Forest' adorned in darkly wonderful scarves. Zarina was twirling around in a gypsy skirt of savage pink, and a turquoise turban, upon which was balanced a crystal ball. But no one's costume really rivalled Tuesday's.

You see she was very much still a child with a slim, willowy frame, but she had such a leading height, she was eye to eye with some adults. And because she was so accustomed to commanding a bear who towered over her, she carried herself like a queen. So it almost didn't matter what you put her in, she drew your heart to her anyway. A timeless girl with untamed curls, and dark, searching eyes. And there was a power to her, a courage that could never be learned.

For this show, Tuesday had been made to look like a music box ballerina, a skirt of swan feathers and a blouse sewn from silver, over which she wore small cape of Arctic fox fur. Zarina had rubbed clove oil through Tuesday's hair, and spent two hours brushing through the curls, before twisting sequins into it so when they caught the light it looked like a crown of snowflakes. But the most magnificent thing about her costume, the thing that stole breath from any audience, and set Tuesday's young soul soaring, was her skates.

They'd been custom-made in Russia from iridescent leather that faded from brilliant white to soft lilac, giving the appearance of being sculpted from glass.

'Five minute call everyone,' piped up Yusef, flouncing across the stage in barely more than jeans, jumper, and a navy blue beret. Tuesday tossed her head from side to side to make sure her hood was secure. Beside her, Promise was dressed like the toy bear, in a silver and gold waistcoat with a little black top hat and rather splendid open-toe black leather skates.

'Got your Cinderella slippers on?' Gretta smiled, though her eyes were fraught with worry as they often were on the final rehearsal. She checked over Tuesday's costume, aggressively unfastening, then re-fastening buttons. Tightening Tuesday's skirt and fiddling roughly with her hair.

'Yes.' Tuesday was so excited about the starlit rehearsal not even Gretta could dampen her mood. 'I love these boots—thank you so much Auntie Gretta.'

Gretta looked her squarely in the eye and spoke with an unexpected softness. 'That's alright love. We used to call you Cinderella. When we found you out on the ice you only had one little boot on.' A small crack pushed its way into Tuesday's heart.

'You mean when Promise found me?'

Gretta's face soured. 'Yes! That's what I said you stupid child.'

Tuesday felt the world grow a little darker and she lowered her gaze, then forced it back up, plastering her smile in place. It didn't really matter, Gretta may have raised her, but she wasn't Tuesday's family. Promise was.

'That's your one minute call,' came Yusef's whiney voice. Gretta sprang away to check Zarina's costume and Jude strode over to Tuesday, a gentle grin upon his serious face.

'Ready?'

'Yep' she answered as Jude opened a huge wooden crate of a box, which had been built on runners like all the other props. Tuesday turned to her bear. 'Promise, in.' He gave a growl of protest slumping down on the frost-covered ice like a huge furry snow angel.

'Lord of the mountains—don't let Gretta see him,' muttered Jude, helping Tuesday heave and tug the docile bear back onto his four feet. 'She'll skin him alive if he ruins another costume.'

'Come on boy,' Tuesday begged, as Promise sauntered away from the open box. He sat down on his haunches and stared at her with such a crestfallen expression that Tuesday had to look away to stop herself giggling. 'Come on my darling,' she smiled. 'It's not that bad, and I'll be in there with you.' Promise hung his head and closed his eyes and Tuesday pressed her forehead to his brow. 'You're my whole world,' she whispered. Jude took a small piece of stale crust out of his pocket and dropped it lightly into the open box.

Promise sniffed the air then padded over, eased

himself up onto his back legs and climbed in as nimbly as a cat. Jude blinked in amazement. 'I didn't know he could move like that.'

Tuesday grinned. 'He's full of surprises.'

Jude peered anxiously into the oblong box. 'Is there enough room in there for you?' he asked uncertainly.

'Yeah, we'll both squash in,' Tuesday assured him, carefully lowering herself in so she was curled on top of Promise, a little bright cherry on a huge white cake.

'Beginners,' Yusef squealed. 'This is your beginners call.'

'Close the lid,' Tuesday urged.

Jude frowned, pursed his lips then did as he'd been asked, listening for the soft click of the catch closing.

Uncle Tolya and several of the acrobats arrived and helped Jude slide the box into position. He squatted down beside it and tapped sharply on the dark wood. A faint little tap came back from inside. 'I'll be in the wings. Any problems just drum on the side.' Another light tap echoed back.

Then the show was starting!

From inside the tight dark vacuum of the box Tuesday heard Uncle Tolya's lilting accordion. There was hardly any air and her world seemed to be made up of thick blackness and the rhythm of Promise's heartbeat. She tried to still her jumping nerves, running through the show in her mind as the clatter of Bressay's hooves pounded the dark ice.

Then the music changed to a jolly little ditty: *Hans and Franco's comedy puppet routine.*

Promise gave a low grumbling moan and one of Tuesday's legs began to go numb. 'Not long now boy,' she soothed, knowing that it was a lie. *I should have asked for a hole to peek out of* she thought, as her mind became cloaked in dizziness. She heard the music change again as Zarina entered the Toyshop and began summoning spirits, then the wild whirling acrobat ice ballet began.

Promise began to fidget angrily. Shifting to and fro, rocking the box from side to side. 'Be still,' Tuesday commanded as she was crushed against the side. But Promise gave a panicked growl which made Tuesday's heart lurch. *My poor bear is frightened.*

He began desperately scrabbling, the blade of one of his skates tearing Tuesday's skirt and slicing at her leg. She balled her fists and thumped on the side trying to get Jude's attention. But Jude couldn't hear her over the music.

With a sickening gasp, Tuesday whirled onto her back and kicked at the lid with her skates, trying to open it. The catch strained and creaked but remained tightly shut. Promise began flailing his claws, catching Tuesday across the cheek. She covered her face, shielding her eyes, kicking at the lid, as if she were fighting for her life. There was the sensation of moving as they were spun by many hands onto stage. 'Get us out,' Tuesday screamed, punching the side of the box and biting back tears.

Suddenly the lid flew open and a horrified Sebastian hauled her out. Tuesday gave a grateful sob, crumpling into his arms. 'My God what's happened?' Sebastian muttered, clutching Tuesday to him. Her face was red with scratches, her swan feather skirt in tatters, and a fast trail of blood streamed down her leg where a deep double gash crossed her shin.

The box crashed to its side, nearly knocking Sebastian and Tuesday over as an enraged Promise thundered out, flailing his back legs wildly until he'd kicked his beautiful skates off. He rose to his full height and began storming around the rink, heading for Yusef and Gretta. Tuesday fought her way out of Sebastian's arms and tried to stand.

'Promise, stop,' she ordered, her voice clear and unshakeably calm. Promise came to a grinding halt in the middle of the black ice, trapped in time by Tuesday's voice. He stood statue-still, and the carnival held their breath. Then he raised his snout to the moon and bellowed, seeming to rock the world.

The *Carnival of Northern Stars* drew back. Lucie began to cry. Zarina rushed forward and laid a gentle hand on Tuesday's shoulder and Jude skated to her side, but Tuesday hardly saw them. All her attention, energy, and spirit were focused on her beautiful distraught bear.

She tried to skate toward him, but the pain in her leg stopped her and she tumbled onto the ice. A little broken doll. As Tuesday's vision swam with stars, Zarina cradled her head and Jude went cautiously to Promise, but didn't touch him.

'Her leg needs stitches,' said Zarina tearfully.

Gretta stormed across the stage glaring at Tuesday furiously. But she knelt down and spoke quietly. 'Zarina can stitch your leg. I'm sure she'll do a lovely job if you just keep still and —'

'No,' interrupted Zarina, looking appalled. 'I'm a seamstress not a nurse. She needs professional help.'

'Nonsense,' Gretta chirped, giving a light little laugh, but a shadow fell over her and she stared up into the ashen face of Anushka.

'You will take the child to see a doctor or my family and I walk from the show tonight. And you will never find a new troupe of acrobats by tomorrow.'

Gretta sucked in a sharp breath through her teeth. 'Who will deal with the bear if Tuesday isn't here?' she growled.

'I'll feed Promise and put him back in his cage,' offered Jude.

Gretta huffed in fierce annoyance. 'Fine. If you want to waste rehearsal time, that's on you. But we open tomorrow night regardless.'

Tuesday felt herself being lifted gently onto one of the sleighs. As the dogs began to race and rush she wasn't aware of much, except the fluttering kiss of falling snow, the strange tug at her bones that happened when Promise was too far away from her. And high up in the sky, the flashing lights of a tiny plane making a slow descent.

Chapter 8

FLY BY NIGHT

From the window of a light aircraft Marv peered down at the deep night snow. Northern winds seemed to scatter the stars and whip up the clouds, letting the pale moon dazzle the ice. Marv pushed the peak of his cap up and squinted. 'Hey look, is that a sleigh?' he said, nudging Sol awake. But by the time Sol peered out of the window, the clouds had swirled back, filling their vision with night.

The plane seemed so small to Marv, and the weather so wild he almost felt as if they were flying on wings of folded paper. Inside it was packed to the roof with both his team and the girls' junior team, and all their kit.

Every now and then the plane would lurch and dive, making some of the kids scream and madly laugh. Marv's dad Leon was up front with Coach, so he felt less jumpy than some of the others. After a while Coach stood and spoke with a levelled calm. 'We'll be landing in fifteen minutes,' he said with a faint hint of a grin. An excited hush swept through the small plane. That was the thing about Coach, his mood when he was happy could lift you up like an ocean wave.

'The next ten days are going to be solid hard work. You're going to have to skate like champions, fight like bears, bring on the miracles.' Marv and Sol fist-bumped, joy quickening their hearts. 'But more than anything look out for each other. We're more than a team. We're family. So be a pack. Any team can have one or two star players, but I want to see six dazzling stars on the ice at all times. Save your stardust when you're on the bench, but the moment your blade touches the ice I want to see you shining.' The kids on the plane gave a cheer of agreement.

'Off the ice your behaviour needs to be impeccable. Or Mr Jackson will be taking you straight home.'

Marv felt his cheeks go hot as Sol gave him a playful shove. 'Yeah, don't upset Mr Jackson, he's really scary.' It was the least true sentence ever spoken. Leon, as all the kids knew, was the biggest softy on the island.'

The plane swooped down then, skidding and screeching across the snow, causing Coach to break a sweat and two of the kids to be sick, one of them being Kobi. Doctor Marilee, who had left the island's surgery in the care of her daughter and was accompanying the team as a favour to Coach, was quick to step in and soothe everyone.

As the two teams piled out, dragging their kitbags, hurrying through the thickly falling flakes, Marv thought he heard the yip of sled dogs and he turned his gaze into the wind, thinking again of the sleigh, but wet falling sleet blocked his view.

The coach from the rival team, a stocky man named Roy had generously come to meet them. He'd brought a regular bright yellow school bus that was set upon enormous tractor wheels so it was elevated from the road. 'Oh yeah, a bear bus!' cried Sol as they jostled their way on. Churchill was one of the few other places that shared its wintery streets with bears. They had come up with clever ways of bear spotting while also staying safe, like the brilliant elevated buses.

'Welcome to Churchill.' Roy shook Coach's hand. 'Good to have you on our side of the ice.'

Marv, Sol, and a few others crowded onto the back of the bus and Leon squeezed in the middle. 'Not all teams do this you know,' said Leon, inclining his head toward the two chatting coaches.

The boys frowned as if they had no idea what he was talking about. 'Our Coach is so well known for what he's done for hockey that everyone respects him.'

Marv and Sol looked at Leon blankly. 'What do you mean?' asked Sol.

Leon chuckled and playfully pulled Sol's cap over his eyes. 'Make it a sport for everyone. Coach was one of the first-ever black players, one of the only black coaches. He's fought all his life off the ice as much as on to give more kids a chance to be part of the game.'

Somewhere at the front of the bear bus a phone rang. Roy answered it and Marv caught a concerned tone: 'For a child? No, no our local doctor's actually away at the moment. I can get one of the nurses . . .' Marv vaguely wondered if one of the players from the opposite team had been hurt. 'A young girl . . . well, how badly? I mean, I can ask the other team's doctor? Yeah, sure I'll get back to you.'

Roy made his way down the bus and spoke swiftly in a lowered voice with Doctor Marilee. 'A young girl's been injured in a skating accident; they've stopped the bleed, but think she might need stitches.'

Doctor Marilee nodded. 'If it's an emergency I could see her in an hour, or tell them to come by the rink first thing tomorrow.' Roy nodded and made a call.

Then the bus was pulling up outside a snug little hotel and everyone was filing out into the wind-whipped night, and all Marv and Sol could think about was hockey, hockey, and hockey.

The next morning Marv woke early, excitement clawing at his heart. He devoured his breakfast and set off through the frozen streets with his dad and

Sol. Their breath turned to ice mist the moment they stepped outside, and deep solid snow crunched under their boots. Marv felt his spirits lift. This was all he wanted to do, play hockey forever and ever. Be part of a team. A family. A pack.

It was 9 a.m. but already the streets of Churchill were bustling with life; tourists were getting coffee before setting out on bear-spotting trips, and—much like on the Isle of Bears—families were making the most of being in the open air in the safety of the light.

Churchill was a town on the brink of the tundra, surrounded by winter-white forest. It always took Marv's breath away to remember just how huge the rest of Canada was and how tiny their island seemed.

They arrived at the rink a few paces behind Coach and Doctor Marilee. Marv smiled warmly at the doctor as she held the door open for him, his moon-mark scar pulling up slightly at the corner of his mouth.

'Morning Jackson, Cooper,' said Coach, his face already focused on the game.

Sol ducked into the locker rooms to phone his mum, Leon went to get coffee, and Coach began assessing the quality of the ice with his slippered feet. Marv settled on a seat breathing in the glorious scent of ice air, daring to imagine the glory that would come if they won. They wouldn't need the plane; their hearts would be so high they'd fly all the way to Winnipeg on happiness alone.

There came a bright, brisk knock at the door. Marv glanced over his shoulder and saw a strange-looking figure lurking outside. 'Just push the door,' he muttered, but she did not. Instead the knock came again more urgently.

Slowly Marv got to his feet and slouched his way over, but Doctor Marilee flitted past him. 'It's alright Marvel,' she said fondly, 'I think they're here for me.'

Marv stepped back as Doctor Marilee opened the door and a woman in some sort of astonishing fur dressing gown swept in.

Her hair was a shock of grey and her eyes so clear they seemed as pale and deathly as ice. But when she addressed Doctor Marilee her whole face softened. 'Are you the doctor?' she said, her accent hard to place and her voice a little shrill. Marv felt unnerved by her, and found himself shrinking back.

Doctor Marilee nodded politely. 'Good. I need you to see to my granddaughter. The silly girl had new skates and managed to nearly slice her own leg off.' The woman chuckled stepping aside and ushering a young girl forward.

Marv pushed his cap up in alarm, for the edge of the girl's skirt had been ripped and stained scarlet, her leg badly bandaged with an ice pack. She was wrapped in a stunning white fur stole and long satin gloves, but as she came in from the cold Marv saw that her skin was deep brown and scattered with scratches of silver.

The same as my scar.

Dark curls spilled from the hood of the girl's cape, and even darker eyes peered out, staring directly at Marv with a sharp intensity. And all of a sudden, his heart was in his throat.

Who is she?

He could see by the look on Doctor Marilee's face that she was equally confused.

Maybe they're in some sort of show or Christmas parade, Marv thought.

Doctor Marilee smiled tightly and beckoned the girl and her wolfskin grandma to follow.

But the injured girl didn't move; instead she stared open-mouthed at Marv. Marv felt his cheeks flush, and feeling a little self-conscious he tilted his cap down, wondering if the brightness of his scar was alarming her, but the girl did not look away. Instead she stumbled toward him, clearly in pain, but determined not to fall. And in that moment, Marv knew that she was a truly gifted skater. For to stand on whisper-thin blades off-ice and not even wobble, despite an injury, meant her balance was impeccable.

She peered at Marv with a questioning frown, cocked her head to one side and said, 'Did the harvest moon paint you golden?'

It was the oddest question Marv had ever been asked.

He realized she must be a lot younger than she looked.

But her face was so serious, so full of hope, that he felt strangely compelled to say yes. Even though he had no idea what she meant. He shrugged a little shyly. 'The harvest moon—' he began, but the wolfskin grandma spoke over him.

'Tuesday, don't be ridiculous! She must be concussed.' The woman wrapped an arm tightly around the child's shoulders and pulled her away.

Tuesday . . . somewhere in his heart a tiny sliver of a memory awoke.

Marv stared after them, feeling utterly bewildered. The door to the little medical room closed and his teammates began filing past him. Marv tried to make sense of his racing thoughts. How old was she? She was almost as tall as him—in skates—yet her face and manner seemed terribly young.

The rink became busy with the hustle and bustle of other players and parents. But Marv blocked them out, his ears straining toward the medical room door.

He put his kit down, tucked his skates under a seat, and found himself walking unexpectedly toward the door and timidly knocking. What was he going to say?

Doctor Marilee opened the door a fraction, and through it Marv saw the girl sitting proudly on the medical bed, as if nothing could hurt her. 'Sol needs a plaster,' Marv muttered, not quite meeting the doctor's eye. It was as good an excuse as any.

'Oh. Sure. Just give me five minutes,' she said, about to close the door; then she seemed to have a sudden change of heart. 'Actually Marvel, you can just grab one from the first aid box,' she said, stepping back a fraction and letting him in.

'This is one of our best players, Marvel,' Doctor Marilee said kindly, as she tended to the girl's bloodied leg. 'Marv knows all about stitches and scars—he once had a run-in with a bear. It's why we call him Marvel.'

Marv ducked his head and fiddled clumsily with the first aid box. The wolfskin grandma smiled at him, but her eyes were so full of cruelty that Marv almost recoiled.

'What did you do to the bear?' asked the girl, staring at Marv incredulously. He felt a rush of nervousness.

'Nothing, I just . . .'

'He went out after dark, alone, when he was very young,' Doctor Marilee explained.

'Out on the ice plains?' the girl's dark eyes were full of questions. And suddenly Marv found himself wanting to tell the truth.

'No, out of my house. I live on an island that we share with bears in the winter . . . One night I thought—'

'How long is this likely to take?' snapped the grandma, glaring at Marv so furiously he at once fell silent.

'Not too long,' answered Doctor Marilee, steadily

stitching the child's leg. 'Do you want to tell me what happened?' she said softly to Tuesday.

'She fell onto the blade of her skate,' barked the grandma.

The girl, Marv noticed, was super brave about having stitches; she seemed not to feel the needle. Marv found a plaster, gave the room a slightly awkward grin and hesitantly left.

Coach appeared and beckoned him to the locker rooms for a team talk. Marv tried with all his might to put the scarred, feathered girl out of his mind. Though it hardly worked. She was impossible to forget. Like a brightness that wouldn't leave his memory.

Or a fragment of a frozen dream.

Chapter 2

A GIRL OF FEATHERS AND SCARS

Once the lovely doctor had finished stitching up the cut, she propped Tuesday's leg up and told her to wait twenty minutes before walking anywhere. Then she graciously excused herself as she had to go see to an ankle sprain of one of the players.

The moment the door to the medical room closed Gretta turned on Tuesday like a storm breaking on a mountain peak. 'What on earth do you think you're doing?' she growled through clenched teeth.

Tuesday swallowed, her little soul aching for her bear. 'I don't . . . What do you mean? I'm not doing anything?' she answered, as truthfully as she dared.

She was finding it hard to breathe without Promise. As if her heart was a compass drawing her north toward him.

Gretta cracked her knuckles furiously. 'You're asking too many questions! Just stay quiet; it's better if you don't speak.' Tuesday felt like she might cry, and she saw Gretta roll her eyes impatiently.

But Tuesday had never been beyond the folds of her carnival before. She had never been anywhere without Promise. Not in all her young wild life. And it felt so daunting without him.

'These aren't carnival folk,' Gretta explained wearily. 'They don't understand us, or our way of life.'

'But that boy looked like me,' Tuesday murmured. 'I thought he might know about the magic of the harvest moon.'

The old woman gave a high-pitched cackle of a laugh. 'Oh Tuesday, you precious thing. A simple boy like him won't know about moon magic.'

Once when she was very small, Tuesday had asked Gretta why she looked different to everyone else in the carnival. Why they were the colour of snow and she was the colour of autumn leaves. Gretta had grinned and cupped Tuesday's small face in her hands. 'The harvest moon painted you golden brown with its warm light so everyone would know you are special.'

Tuesday had accepted this with delight.

But now she suddenly doubted this. She suddenly doubted everything.

Gretta gave a long sigh and then spoke more tenderly. 'We are a carnival made from hard work and mystical acts; we do extraordinary things that no one else is capable of. There is no one else in the world who can ice skate with a ruddy beast of a polar bear.'

As she said this Gretta moved nearer and took hold of Tuesday's little gloved hand. 'You are truly a miraculous girl, Moonrise Tuesday, and these people will never understand that.'

Tuesday nodded and gave Gretta a fleeting smile.

'That is why you must never leave *North Star*, Tuesday, not ever. Do you understand me love?'

Tuesday felt the world tilt.

Does Gretta know I sometimes dream of running away?

She sat up very suddenly. She missed *North Star*. She missed her bear. She missed the ice. 'I want to go home,' she said in a small voice.

It was very unlike her and made Gretta wonder if she really was concussed, or at least dazed. 'Alright darling, as soon as this silly game's over we'll get going. There's too many people outside – we'll go when it's calmed down.'

'What is the game?' asked Tuesday, listening to the growing din outside the door.

'Oh, it's a stupid thing called hockey. Don't concern yourself with it love, there's no grace to it.'

Tuesday rubbed her eyes. 'Auntie Gretta may I have

some water please?' To Tuesday's surprise Gretta nodded.

'Stay right here and I'll get you some,' she said. Gretta was unsure about whether to leave Tuesday, but could acknowledge that the child looked remarkably faint. Gretta gave the girl a lovely, lasting smile and Tuesday could not keep from smiling back. Just for a moment it was like she was little again and Gretta was her world and they were out together on the ice at sunset, holding hands and paws with Promise.

Promise.

Tuesday was alone, as Gretta left the medical room. She clutched at her chest trying to soothe her battered heart. She felt shadowless without Promise. She tried not to listen for his snuffling, or seek out his huge white shape, or feel his breath in her hair. Yet she heard and felt and saw him anyway, as if the distance between them was nothing but a footstep, as if he were simply waiting for her on the other side of the door. And she knew then, just as sharply as she had always known, that she could never live without him. He was her world, where he went, she would follow. If he stayed in the carnival, she would stay too. If he left, she would leave with him, even if it meant living in an eternal winter.

She thought of the boy—Marvel. He had said that he came from an island shared between people and bears. 'Maybe there is a place for us after all,' she whispered, speaking to Promise as if he were beside her.

Outside the door, Tuesday sensed a darkening of light, a ceasing of sound, and she hobbled to the door and pushed it a little way open. She couldn't leave—Gretta would hit the roof—but she could at least have a peek at this strange thing they called hockey. And maybe if she could find Marvel, he might tell her where this mysterious island was.

The rink had fallen into a simmering, whispering darkness. Tuesday balanced on the jagged tip of her ice skates gazing out across one of the biggest indoor rinks she'd ever seen.

She normally despised indoor skating, but here the air felt charged with energy, like she could almost taste the excitement. Two huge spotlights circled around the ice. *Is it a show?* Then a fierce drumming started up that seemed to pound the walls and floor. The lights flared, the crowd roared, and all around her Tuesday felt a swirl of feverish joy take hold. She saw clusters of families all dressed in identical colours. There were banners and flags hanging from the roof and an overpowering smell of fresh sausages and hope.

Tuesday crept forward craning to see as music began to blare. Two lines of boys skated out from a sort of secret tunnel. *Backstage!* Tuesday thought gleefully. *It is a show.*

But the boys weren't in real costumes; they were all

dressed in bulky kit that padded their bodies and hid their faces. 'But how can they skate like that? How can they leap or twirl? ' she said, accidentally speaking to Promise.

Tuesday saw that their skates were different to hers. They seemed huge, so chunky, with blades like daggers. *Why are they holding sticks?* Then a terrifying alarm sounded and Tuesday saw why.

Something small and black, like a ball but flatter, shot across the ice, and the boys flew fast as husky-drawn sleighs across the rink, whacking at the thing with sticks. Only the sticks weren't made of wood; they were shiny, metallic.

At first Tuesday had no idea what was happening except that everyone seemed to chase the black thing up and down the ice. Two boys collided in front of her, hurtling into the boards with a whack that set her bones on edge.

Everyone else on the ice seemed to still, dropping their sticks or holding them high. The audience rose to their fee; Tuesday felt herself tilt forward along with the crowd.

She saw a boy with merciless eyes, red hair peeking from the sides of his helmet, glare at a far bigger boy. They circled each other like two savage sharks drawing closer and closer. The red-haired boy struck the blond boy in face. Tuesday gasped, her hands flying to her mouth in shock. The other boy fought back, whacking and pummelling him, but to her amazement the red-haired kid turned and ducked and did a small dance around the bigger boy, making the crowd howl and giggle. Then he swerved to a breathtakingly beautiful stop and bowed to his audience.

Gretta was wrong, this game is full of grace. Full of skill. Full of battle. 'It's a carnival!' she cried, and a man in the stands beside her laughed and replied: 'It sure is.'

Tuesday had been raised upon ballet and berries and the love of her bear. 'Eat little, train lots, practise, practise, practise, and always, always be graceful, even off the ice.' Stand with a straight back, a raised chin, and a delicate poise. But never had Tuesday seen people skate with the brutal, darting courage of hockey players, and all at once she wanted to do it—to be part of the action.

The small black thing skimmed and bounced over the ice and flew into a little net, and all around Tuesday people began hugging each other and cheering. On the ice, one team all flocked around a smallish boy, congratulating him. He raised the cage of his helmet to wipe his brow and Tuesday's mouth fell open. The boy with the bear-scar. Marvel.

And what a heart-stopping skater he was. So nimble in those huge heavy skates. Seeming to run like a ballerina.

The game started up again but Tuesday barely noticed the other players, her eyes only following Marvel. Maybe if she found where the dressing rooms were, she could wait for him afterwards.

But Gretta will be back soon.

Tuesday found herself wrestling with her own will. She didn't want to upset Gretta. Things would be tense enough with the rehearsal time they'd already lost.

An island of bears. Maybe Promise could live there—with me . . .

This was her chance. Tuesday peered around wildly, her eyes honing in on a fur-clad figure on the other side of the rink, slowly picking her way through the rows of seats.

What's she doing? Tuesday wondered, as she watched Gretta hover by each seat and lay something on it. Then with a sharp realization she understood. Gretta was flyering, advertising the carnival. Tuesday measured the distance between them—if she was quick, there should just be enough time. She hoped.

Behind her she became aware of a horn sounding, the game stopping as abruptly as it had started, and the ice clearing. People began leaving their seats. *Is it the end?* She stared around nervously and saw that no one was leaving, but folk were queuing up to buy hotdogs and soda. *No, it must be the interval.*

And she set off, as subtly as she could manage, trying

to hide her limp, and moved toward the little tunnel that the players were vanishing into.

But being indoors made Tuesday's heart race, and she was swiftly aware of a million eyes staring at her. It was then that she noticed how differently she was dressed to everyone else. They were all wearing jeans and jerseys. She looked like a bedraggled Canada goose. How she wished she could pluck the bloodied feathers away.

A group of older girls with a large bag of cotton candy gaped at Tuesday then started whispering. A swirling terror took hold of her and she fought the urge to flee, sweat shimmering on her brow. She drew herself up straighter, fighting to keep calm. *I'm a performer* she told herself, forcing her chin upwards, and walked around the edge of the rink. Though beneath her cape she was shaking.

It was all taking so long, and with every step her balance almost failed her. Tuesday couldn't see a way to the dressing rooms, and turning abruptly on her skates, she could no longer see the medical room. Fear clawed at her throat, and she bit down on a lock of her hair not to cry, when an extremely tall man with night-dark skin and fur slippers, crossed her path and opened a doorway she hadn't noticed.

Tuesday had never seen anyone who looked as wonderful as him and for a moment she was too star-struck to move. Then she steadied herself and slipped through the closing door.

Tuesday found herself in a small, badly-lit corridor full of echoes. At once she clapped her hands over her nose in disgust; the smell was unbearable. And Tuesday lived with a bear!

What is that?

She thought of the thick kit the boys wore and how fast they skated and how hot she felt just standing still, and realized it was the smell of sweat and adrenalin. It was awful.

But she moved forward all the same, hoping against hope she'd be able to find Marvel.

A voice deep as thunder, cut through the din. 'Are you OK there miss? Are you lost?' Tuesday turned and gazed up into the face of the man in fur slippers. His age was hard to place; something about him seemed almost timeless, and his eyes were deep and inquisitive.

Tuesday swallowed.

'I'm looking for—' she began, but a fur-clad figure swept briskly around the corner.

'Tuesday!' Gretta hissed, 'I told you to wait in the medical room.'

Tuesday visibly jumped, almost falling over. 'I was . . . I was scared without you,' she lied.

The man in fur slippers stared hard at Gretta, but said nothing.

Gretta scowled, pushed a bottle of water into Tuesday's hands, then took her by the wrist and hurried her away. Back through the hidden door, back past the gawking crowds, back around the edge of the glistening rink.

Tuesday glanced back just once as she was pulled toward the outside world. And there by the medical room staring after her was the boy called Marvel.

He came to find me . . .

She reached out, gave a fleeting wave, and just for a moment their eyes met and Marvel moved toward her.

Did he call her name? Tuesday couldn't tell. Then the door to the rink closed and Tuesday and Gretta were rushing through winter-white streets, back through the trees to the sea ice where the little sleigh and the dogs were hidden. She felt pulled in two directions. One part of her ached to see Promise. The other wished she could go back and speak to the boy.

But it was too late. The boy with the bear-scar was gone.

Chapter 10

THE BEAR IN THE BOX

Marv stood in perfect stillness, staring as the girl in swan feathers vanished out of the door.

He had missed her. Tuesday had gone.

Whoever she was.

In that strange heartbeat of a moment when she'd waved at him, Marv had felt as if they were staring at each other across the ice and years and falling snow, and he couldn't shake the sense that it was just like his dream.

He turned dejectedly back toward the locker rooms. 'You're doing well out there son, keep it up.' Leon fell in step beside Marv as he clomped back to the locker rooms. 'So, afterwards, I've found something that might be of interest.'

'Oh yeah?' asked Marv, wondering if his dad had found a new pizza place.

'Do you remember that circus you mentioned on your birthday?'

Marv's heart began to boom in his ears. 'Yes,' he breathed.

'Look at this,' said Leon, delicately slipping something into Marv's gloved hands.

It was a flyer advertising a circus of some sort. Across the top were the words *The Carnival of Northern Stars.*

And on the front like an illustration from a fairy tale was a gorgeously sketched picture of a girl dancing with a bear.

The bear, with its silvery-white fur and violet collar looked as if it were jauntily prancing. The girl looked luminous, soaring forward in a high arabesque, the colourful stripes of a carnival tent behind her.

She looks like . . . Tuesday . . .

Marv thought of the cut on her leg. Of her fairy tale costume. He absolutely had to know if it was her. 'Can we go to the carnival?' Marv gasped.

'We'll see,' said Leon. 'Now, get out there and win!'

'But Dad . . . we have to go.'

A note of desperation crept into Marv's voice and Leon turned to look at him. 'I think she was here, this same girl. I think I just met her.' Leon peered at Marv hard and frowned. 'I bet she's an incredible skater,' Marv added keeping his tone light.

'Alright son, if you want to see the circus then I guess

I can make it happen.'

Marv gave his dad a firm hug. 'It's a carnival Dad, but whatever. Thanks.'

The rest of the game passed in a rush, and Marv knew he had to be professional and put the strange carnival and the strange girl out of his mind.

He just about managed it, but it was tough. The exquisite image from the flyer kept fluttering through his mind.

Then Kobi got sent off for hurting one of the other team with his stick. And without Kobi to protect them, both Marv and Sol got harmed by the opposition, not badly, but wounded enough not to play.

They lost 3-5 to Churchill. Coach was calm but not so silently disappointed in Kobi, and though the red-headed boy carried on as if he was unaffected, Marv thought he saw a flicker of shame cross his face.

As soon as the third period was over, Marv began tearing off his kit and pulling on his coat and dragging a slightly-confused Sol along with him.

'Dad, we're ready to go!'

Leon who had been studying the flyer shook his head. 'There's no show today Marv, and you've got training all day tomorrow.'

'But we have to . . .'

Leon gave a sorry sigh. 'I just don't think it's going to happen this year.'

'But that's the thing, Dad. The carnival is, like, mysterious. Rae said they just arrive in the middle of the night and take off again. There might not be another time. If there really is a girl who skates with a bear, wouldn't that be amazing to see?' Leon did not look convinced.

'I would definitely like to watch this weird show,' put in Sol. 'Or at least find where the tents are pitched.'

'I just want to say hi, see if she's OK,' added Marv.

Roy approached and shook both the young players' hands. 'Good game out there,' he said gruffly.

'Do you know how to get to this ice show thing?' asked Sol brightly.

Roy studied the flyer. 'Yeah, I know this carnival; they visited once before, long time ago. Quite strange. I expect they're just off the coast. I could drive you to the shore.'

Leon began to shake his head, but Marv grabbed Roy's hand and spoke up: 'Yes. That would be awesome and very kind of you.'

Half an hour later they were piling onto a bear bus, heading for the edge of the land, where the town turned to tundra, then the pale frozen sea.

'I'll be back in an hour,' called Roy in a warm voice. And then Marv, Sol, and Leon were skating somewhat cautiously (Leon in borrowed skates) over the snow-white ice sheets, a tense, breathing silence falling over them all.

Leon had his phone and set of binoculars with him to keep a lookout for roaming polar bears. But so far so good.

A sound came, carried on the wind. The yip and howl of huskies. Marv darted forward. Something was brightly glimmering on the horizon, about half a mile away. 'Is that it?' he asked. 'Are they wagons?'

Leon and Sol followed his gaze.

'They sure are,' said Leon, sounding as astonished as his son.

For there in the distance under a snow-cloud sky was a carnival of colours and dreams. At two o'clock, the Arctic light was already fading, but as they got nearer Marv saw it was an encampment of wonderful wagons set up around a makeshift stage. In the centre a large red and white tarpaulin was strung up over a seating area where small fires had been built. Beyond that was a stage of black ice.

But there was no audience yet. Instead, the carnival seemed to be in the midst of a serious rehearsal.

'That's close enough,' said Leon, laying a hand on both boys' shoulders. 'Your mom would kill me if she knew we'd even come this far.'

'OK, but when they're done can we say hi?' Marv begged.

Marv stared through the binoculars and caught

sight of the wolfskin grandma, but she and a few other sombre-looking figures all had their backs to him, their attention focused upon a tall boy on stage with an ebony pony.

He handed the binoculars to Sol. They were close enough that he could see the show anyhow.

Folk music began echoing across the ice from a lilting accordion, and all three of them raised their caps to watch. The tall boy's skating was breathtaking. It wasn't quite figure skating, or ice dancing, as the jumps he did weren't tricks Marv could name, and there was a chaos to the performance. It was a whole other level of showmanship.

The music changed key, the stage began swirling with eerie mist. Marv rubbed his eyes, not wanting to miss anything, then he frowned as the boy and pony exited and a huge box slid into place.

'Is this a magic show?' joked Sol. 'What do you think's in there?'

The box sprang open. All three of them gasped as Tuesday in a gown of white, rose doll-like from the box. Marv's hand flew to his mouth. 'But she only just had stitches,' he breathed.

Tuesday climbed carefully out of the box. There was a long pause. The music stilled, snowflakes whirled and the wolfskin woman shouted something they couldn't hear. The girl turned delicately to the box as if beckoning someone from within.

'Is there someone else in there?' Leon mumbled.

A terrible coldness took hold of Marv's bones. *Surely you couldn't fit a . . .*

And then the impossible became real, as a black snout appeared, then a huge majestic ice bear roared to his feet.

Leon almost dropped the binoculars. Sol cried out in bewilderment and Marv gave a gasp so sharp he almost inhaled ice.

'But that can't be right,' Leon half yelled.

'W-w-wow is this even happening?' Sol was stammering, but Marv wasn't listening, for in that moment his entire universe seemed to consist of Tuesday and her bear.

The bear growled in protest and Marv's heart ached for him. *He didn't want to be in that box . . .*

The bear stumbled gracelessly out of the box, gnashing its teeth in what seemed like fury.

Leon swore, Sol stumbled backwards, Marv moved forward, his heart roaring in his ears. The wolfskin woman grabbed a poker from one of the small fires and began brandishing it wildly in the direction of the bear.

The bear rose onto its hind legs, with surprising balance, and Marv saw that his hind feet were in huge bladed sandals . . . *Skates.*

The bear gave a terrible, rageful roar and Marv

lurched over the ice—he couldn't stand still and watch this. Surely the bear would attack Tuesday. He knew how vicious bears could be. He had to help her. But Leon grabbed hold of him, keeping him back.

Upon the stage Tuesday stood statue-still, completely unafraid. She glided closer to the bear and melted into him, throwing her arms around his neck in a gesture so tender, everyone stopped breathing.

Leon, who had gathered both Marv and Sol into a protective grasp, gave a strangled sigh as gradually the bear calmed, and after a moment or two stood still of his own accord.

Sweat speckled Leon's skin, as he took in the huge claws, the feral teeth, the dazzle of his sequined waistcoat, the massively bizarre skates fastened to the bear's feet; the child beside him. It was like watching a macabre fairy tale, part nightmare, part miracle.

The wolfskin woman lowered the heated pole and at once a merry little tune began.

'What? Are they just going to keep performing?' muttered Marv. For it seemed they were.

Tuesday gave a mechanical shake of her shoulders, the tattered feather skirt was long gone, a cloak of snow leopard fur now swirling at her shoulders all the way down to her ankles. Her dark curls, shot through with silver ribbons spilled from beneath her hood. She rose onto the jagged ice-pick of her skates and paraded in a marionette-like manner to one side of the stage.

Opposite her the bear did the same. Tuesday slipped off her long cape, a golden figure skater's costume catching the stage lights so she looked like a girl cut from starlight. Marv felt his mouth fall open as the tempo picked up and Tuesday moved as fluidly as silk toward her bear, leapt with a heaven-sent grace into the air, extending her small hands toward him. Astonishingly, the bear caught her in a perfect swan lift, then she slipped through his grip soft as feathers and began to skate seamlessly backwards.

As Marv watched the world disappeared, the ice and snow fell away, the seasons vanished: Tuesday was all Marv could see, a rising moon, lighting the sky.

A brown girl, dancing with a bear. It was an echo of his dream. All he could think of was the baby in the basket with her jewel-bright eyes. The cub on the frozen River Raven, with a wild wintery soul.

It has to be them. It has to be her.

'We have to find out who she is.'

'We have to get her away from that bear is what we have to do,' said Leon, wiping sweat from his brow despite the cold.

As they watched her dance, it seemed that Tuesday saw them too and she paused, mid-spin, staring across the ice directly at Marv before whirling away. The wolfskin woman's head snapped around and she glowered in their direction and began barking orders. The music bluntly stopped. The tall boy who had skated with the pony, came to help lead the bear away. A group of other performers fussed around Tuesday, rushing her off the stage as a man in a rabbit skin jacket, a beret, and suede boots came striding over the ice. His movements harried, his eyes gleaming a little too enthusiastically.

'Welcome, welcome,' he simpered. 'We're not open yet, but the show starts tomorrow at 4.30 if you'd like to purchase tickets.' Marv instinctively didn't like him.

'We'd like that very much,' said Leon smoothly, folding his arms.

'Wonderful,' the man half cooed, pulling out a ticket roll from his pocket.

'It's quite an act you've got there,' Leon continued, slowly getting his wallet.

'Who is that awesome girl?' babbled Sol. 'Is that like a real polar bear? Like a real actual bear with sequins and skates. I mean it's incredible.'

'A star attraction,' the rabbit fur man simpered. *Moonrise Tuesday and Winter's Promise.*

'Her parents must be pretty brave folk, letting her skate with a bear like that,' Leon commented, counting out his money.

The man said nothing but smiled coldly.

'Are they bear trainers?' asked Marv, choosing his words carefully. 'I mean where do the family come from?' Though he was sure of the answer already: *We found the baby and the cub on a frozen river.*

'Tuesday's grandmother raised her and the bear together. She's the true trainer,' the man went on.

Marv closed his eyes, remembering the figure in the long coat he thought he had seen that night long ago. So there had been someone else there: the wolfskin grandma.

Leon frowned deeply and handed over some cash.

'First time it's ever been done,' the man boasted.

'What about Tuesday—like, when did she start skating with a bear?' asked Sol.

The man gave him a tight grin. 'We are a carnival of magic and mystery.'

'Well, we look forward to the show,' Leon said, quickly taking the tickets and turning to leave.

'Why is she called Tuesday?' asked Marv, his voice barely louder than breath.

'It's her lucky day,' the man smiled, though there was no joy in it. Then he was gone, sauntering away as casually as if the ice were fields of summer grass.

Marv, Sol, and Leon were silent for some moments, all staring at each other in bewildered shock.

'Tuesday's my lucky day too,' said Marv quietly, as they began skating back toward the tundra.

'Yeah right,' laughed Sol.

'It is so. Tuesday was the day of the bear attack, when

the islanders saved my life and Doctor Marilee stitched my face up.'

The day I saw a baby and cub together on the River Raven, Marv thought, letting the unspoken words hang in the air.

Though he didn't see it, behind Marv Leon kept glancing back at the carnival, where a wooden box stood upon a black ice stage, and a hot poker rested in a burning fire. And Leon's face became grave with concern.

Chapter 11

COLDER THAN EVER BEFORE

Thick winter-spun twilight gathered around the three wind-whipped skaters as they made their way back to Roy's bus. Marv felt the shift in shadows, the rising darkness seeming to match their mood.

'How was it?' Roy asked on the bumpy drive back to the hotel. 'Did you see the girl?'

'There's something not quite right about the whole thing,' Leon muttered, and no one else spoke for the rest of the journey though the air seemed to flicker with unasked questions.

The image of Tuesday emerging from the box, followed by a huge white-wintered bear, played through Marv's mind like a moment from a dream he couldn't forget.

Back at the hotel, although there were skates to clean, kit to be aired, and fun to be had in the small games room, Marv's mind remained on the carnival. Soon enough, he and Sol found themselves sneaking away up to their room, whispering amongst themselves about the strange afternoon they'd had.

'We totally have to bring our phones tomorrow so we can film the carnival,' Sol chattered, but another voice reached Marv through the wall and he was suddenly on his feet, pressing his ear to it, signalling to Sol to hush.

Sol was so used to reading Marv's body language on the ice he instantly fell silent and leaned into the wall to listen beside him.

In the next room Leon was speaking in a low tone.

'I don't know who her family are, but no child, professional or otherwise, should be risking her life like that for a show.'

'The grandma didn't mention any parents, but she seemed to care an awful lot about the girl,' put in Doctor Marilee softly.

'To let her skate after an injury—with a polar bear . . .' Leon half hissed.

'The brown girl in skates?' Coach's voice asked.

Marv could only suppose his dad nodded as Coach continued speaking. 'Yeah, I saw that girl with that wolfish grandma and I didn't warm to the woman. I knew I'd seen her before, but I couldn't think where, but now I reckon I've got it.'

'Where?' Marv and Sol mouthed to each other.

'I think this carnival visited the island years ago. I took a group of kids from the rink to see it. Long while back. Kobi was there.'

Marv felt a sweeping coldness rush over his skin as if the north wind was in the room with them.

The carnival had been to the island.

'When?' he whispered. But Sol could only shrug.

'They're pretty smart from what I can tell,' put in Leon. 'The whole thing's pitched off the land, on the ice, so technically they're not in anyone's territory.'

Marv didn't quite know what this meant, but he guessed it implied the carnival didn't have to answer to anyone.

'I'm going to speak to Roy, find out if anyone knows anything about the carnival's history or the girl's family,' said Doctor Marilee, and there came the click of the door closing, as the adults dispersed.

'If we could just find out when the carnival came to the island . . .' Marv sighed.

Sol peered at him closely. 'Why?' Marv didn't know how to answer. It seemed ridiculous to speak his jumbled thoughts out loud. But this was Sol. His best friend.

Marv sat down on the edge of the bed and stared at his wiggling toes. 'Because maybe . . .' The words stuck in Marv's throat, his mouth going dry. He swallowed, steadied his mind like he did moments before a game, then tried again. 'What if . . . they, like, stole a baby and a bear cub and trained them to skate together.'

Marv winced a little, waiting for the teasing sound of Sol's laughter. Instead Sol grabbed him by the shoulders: 'Let's ask Coach!'

But Marv shook his head. 'We can't; then he'll know we were listening in on him.'

'Then let's ask someone else who was there—I mean what about Kobi?'

Marv stiffened. Things between him and Kobi were reasonably OK. Good even, so long as they worked together on the ice, kept out of each other's way on land.

'Remember what Rae said on Halloween!' Sol pressed. *If the girl and bear had grown up together, they'd have a special respect for each other. That's the only way it could work.*

The words seemed to swirl around Marv's mind like morning mist, and he found himself agreeing, standing up, and following Sol out of their room.

Kobi's room was two floors up, but the climb felt like it took two years. With every step Marv's heart got louder in his ears, and by the time they reached the door he could hear nothing else but his own doubts and drumming panic.

He thought of his meeting with Tuesday. The way she'd been hurried out of the rink, the way she had seemed to reach out to him. The way she had risen out of the box, quite fearless.

He raised his fist and pounded on the door. There was a moment of stillness. Marv and Sol held their breath. Then it flew dramatically open and Kobi leaned out, a skate clutched in one hand, the silver blade catching the light.

Marv peered down awkwardly noticing how bruised Kobi's bare feet were. His skates must be way too small, Marv realized.

'What' up bear-fighter?'

'We need to ask you something random,' Sol cut in. Kobi raised an eyebrow. 'It's about your childhood—kind of,' Sol went on, slightly losing his way.

Kobi sniggered, but Marv thought his eyes got colder, sadder somehow.

'There's this carnival we went to today just off the ice.' Marv showed Kobi the flyer.

'Excellent. A girl who dances with a bear! What, are you hoping to join them or something Jackson, run away with the circus? Fight bears for a living?'

Marv ignored the jibe and kept talking. 'Coach thinks it's the same carnival he took you and some of the team to when you were much younger.'

Kobi frowned now, and snatched the flyer off Marv. 'Nope. Don't recognize it.'

'But do you remember seeing a show? With Coach? Can you remember when it was?' Kobi huffed impatiently and Marv fought the urge to draw back from him.

'What is this about Jackson? What do you even care?'
His voice had turned icy cool. 'What are you, like, jealous
Coach didn't take you?' he asked, leaning forward, the
skate slightly raised. 'You get everything. The family.
The new gear, any time your stick breaks you get a new
one! And you're *still* jealous.' He snorted. 'You weren't
even on the team then. You weren't the Marvel—no
one even knew you. It was before that bear got shot
and—' he broke off and shoved Marv backwards into
the opposite wall. Sol drew a sharp breath.

Marv pushed away from the wall and stepped closer
to Kobi, surprising them both. 'You saw the carnival
before the bear attack?' he asked, his voice somehow
calm, clear.

Kobi narrowed his eyes. 'Yep. Reckon it was around
the same day—and they didn't have any dancing bears,
so whatever this is just get over it already.' He vanished
back into his room slamming the door in their faces.

Marv had gone still and beside him Sol was gaping,
unable to keep his wide-eyed expression to himself.

'Man, why does he hate you so much?' murmured Sol
as they stumbled away. Marv was about to shrug when
Kobi's words sunk in.

The supportive family. The new kit. The stardom.

'Kobi doesn't have any of the good stuff,' said Marv.
'Hockey is it for him. His shot to be great at something.
His kit's always, like, knackered; he doesn't even wear

half of it.' Marv trailed off thinking of the day in the rink at the beginning of training when Kobi had skated without a helmet.

Was it too small?

'So, like, if you hadn't become Marvel, Kobi would have had all the sponsorship?' asked Sol.

'Guess so', breathed Marv as they reached their room.

🌲 🌲 🌲

Marv couldn't keep still. He ran through all the facts.

'The carnival visited the island around the night of the bear attack. There was no bear or dancing girl. That night a baby and a bear cub vanish. Now the carnival has an ice skating bear who dances with a girl who looks like the baby.' He paused staring at Sol. 'Do you think that's enough to go on.'

'Yes!' cried Sol. 'Tell your dad. Or Coach—someone!'

Marv was giddy with possibility. *What if it really is her?*

'Yeah. I will. I'll catch them both at dinner.'

Sol began nattering away, unlacing and re-lacing his skates.

Marv felt restless. He moved to the window gazing across a world made wild by winter. *Somewhere out there was Tuesday.*

The sky over Hudson Bay was dark and starry, the

moon a single gleaming pearl. Marv still had Leon's binoculars from earlier, and he squinted through them wondering if he might see the blaze of the carnival's fires on the horizon. But there was nothing. Nothing but the night and all its secrets. Nothing at all, but endless black ice.

Marv bit the side of his cheek, wondering if he was looking in the right direction, and as he turned his head tilting the binoculars west, a burning streak of light caught his eye. Marv peered hard: it was like watching a formation of shooting stars streaming over the ice. Then with a sudden gaping coldness Marv understood what he was seeing.

'No! They're leaving! Sol—get my dad now!'

Both boys crashed down the stairs, into the little dimly-lit bar where Leon, Doctor Marilee, Roy, and Coach were sat talking in low voices.

'The carnival's leaving. It's moving on already!'

Leon stood up and bolted to the window.

'So it is,' he said, shaking his head in disbelief.

'They must have sensed something,' said Doctor Marilee.

'Guess they didn't like you asking too many questions,' sighed Coach, who was leaning toward the glass frowning.

'Is keeping a polar bear illegal?' gasped Sol.

'It's extremely dangerous,' said Doctor Marilee. 'We

all know what bears are capable of,' and here she darted a look at Marv.

'Yeah . . . I know,' Marv cut in. 'It's not a normal bear though . . . ' He tried not to blush as everyone in the room turned to him. 'I mean that bear, when they skated together it was like watching magic. It was like they belonged together. Or had grown up together . . . '

Leon put an arm around his son's shoulders. 'I know,' he said gently. 'A real ice bear miracle.'

'There'll be a way to trace the carnival . . . somehow,' Doctor Marilee said, seeing how forlorn Marv looked.

'People always leave something behind,' said Coach, and he held out a single white feather, sleek as the wing of a swan.

Marv felt the vanishing of the carnival far more deeply than any loss he'd ever known.

There had been a baby. There had. And a cub, and here they were in *The Carnival of Northern Stars*, but still out of reach.

It was hours before he even got close to sleep.

And though Marv didn't know it, beyond his windows, over the tundra and across ice the colour of midnight, Tuesday knelt up in her sled-wagon, her hands gripping the bars, as she stared fiercely out wondering if she would ever see the boy with the bear-scar again.

It was rare for Yusef to cancel a show, but it happened from time to time. Sometimes audience members became completed enchanted by Tuesday and wanted to know everything about her, and in the night the carnival and its brightest star would quietly disappear.

At other times the weather was so treacherous that no one could make the journey to see them, though Yusef lit all the lamps and opened the show anyway, but they would stop if no one had arrived by the end of the first dance, and move on unafraid of the winter.

Tuesday had never known them leave an encampment simply on a whim or worry. *But what are we running from?*

She chewed on a tendril of night-dark hair, trying to thread all her thoughts together.

Marvel had come to *North Star;* Tuesday had seen him. He was far in the distance, but she'd known it was him. Had he come to speak to her? To help her? Had he somehow frightened Yusef?

She was relieved not to have to perform a full show so soon after stitches, but she wished she could have spoken to Marvel.

Beside her, Promise dosed and snorted, his great head resting heavily in her lap. A constant weight to anchor her in a world of spinning ice and uncertainties.

Tuesday rubbed his ears and thought again of Marvel's island. *Is there really a place where people and bears live side by side?* Tuesday hoped with every sharp bone in her body that there was. She wilted against

Promise and fell at last into a dreamless sleep.

As the huskies drew to a reluctant stop, Tuesday sat up, rubbed her eyes and found she needed to move, to look for answers. She took the key from her pocket and unlocked the wagon door and slipped out, softly as a snowflake.

Promise lumbered out behind her and they went for their morning wander. Girl and bear moving in step, a silvery thread of silent thoughts weaving its way between them.

Performers rose sleepily and peeped out of sledwagons, and those who'd been up driving the dogs all night crept gratefully to bed.

There would be no show today.

Everyone turned to smile at Tuesday as she went by. Zarina came bursting out of her wagon and swept her into a hug, even gave her a small purse of lavender to help soothe her bear. 'Put it under his pillow when he sleeps, and sprinkle a little in the box so he feels at ease when he has to climb in.' Tuesday could have wept with gratitude. But she did not; she held herself together and smiled her thanks.

'Morning Tuesday,' Hans and Franco grinned, passing her a small warm clay mug filled with creamy, sugary tea. It tasted heavenly. 'How's that leg doing?' they asked in cheerful voices, seemingly unafraid of Gretta chiding them for being too soft on Tuesday.

'It's fine.' Tuesday nodded politely, as they gave Promise a long slurp of tea too.

Uncle Tolya opened his wagon door and leaned his whiskey-pale face into the day. He'd been up all night driving. Sleep and icicles coated his eyelashes and he looked as he was already half in a dream, but he came toward Tuesday now, nearer than he'd ever been to her while she was with Promise, and he threw something around her shoulders. It was a large scarf, or a small blanket of fine-spun pink wool. 'It's so good to see you're doing OK,' he said kindly, taking hold of Tuesday's gloved hands.

'Of course I'm OK.' Tuesday shrugged. And it was true, she was sad to leave Churchill, but this warm display of kindness, this welcome feeling of acceptance from the company of *North Star* made a little of the ice in Tuesday's heart melt away. She wasn't used to such affection.

'We were all so worried when you got stuck in that box . . . ' He broke off here, and Tuesday was amazed to see him wipe a tear from a misty eye. 'I've known you since you were a babe, since Gretta brought you in from the cold wrapped in this blanket.' He indicated the shawl around Tuesday's shoulders. 'I kept it for you, all this time. You are truly part of the carnival Tuesday, but whoever left you out on the ice . . . ' He faltered for a moment looking nervous. 'Well, wherever you came from, you were loved.'

Tuesday was silent. It was rare to have something so precious that was her own, that had come from before.

The acrobat children who were already wide awake and cartwheeling all over the roof of their wagon called to Promise in sing-song voices, beckoning Tuesday over. This never happened; normally they were too wary of the bear.

Peering inside, Tuesday had never seen such a delightfully messy little nook before. The walls were adorned with flowers and creatures Tuesday couldn't name. There were symbols depicted across the ceiling which she knew to be letters, though she couldn't read them. Sequinned scarves were hung across the windows, and crammed into every breathable space were fabulous hand-carved wooden toys.

Tuesday had never had any toys—not really. Promise always accidentally destroyed them.

'Come in,' Anushka smiled, but Tuesday found she could not leave Promise's side. They were a unit. A team. A family. And there was no room for Promise in the warm and wonderful acrobat wagon.

'OK, my little love,' said Anushka settling on the steps outside, Lucie clambering all over her lap. She handed Tuesday a warm baked apple, and Lucie playfully tossed another to the bear. It was cold, but lovely.

Tuesday took a small breath. 'Why are we fleeing?'

she asked softly.

Anushka frowned a little, but answered. 'Those people who came to the rehearsal yesterday, well, whoever they were, Yusef didn't like them.'

'I met one of them at the ice rink; he was there when I had my stitches.'

Anushka's frown deepened. 'Tuesday, you are such a gifted girl, this show could not exist without you . . . But the rest of us . . . we may not always be here . . . '

Tuesday felt as if the fabric of her world was being pulled apart. The acrobat family had been with the carnival some three years. She had grown to love them, to think of them like cousins. 'Why?' she gasped.

Anushka lowered her voice. 'Some of us are uncomfortable with the way Gretta and Yusef do things.' She paused and stroked Tuesday's face. 'And the way they treat you, my love, and your bear.'

Tuesday gulped awkwardly, trying to remain composed. 'If you leave . . . will you take us with you?' she stuttered in a small, shocked voice.

Anushka gave a deep sigh and gripped Tuesday's hands. 'Oh Tuesday . . . we cannot bring you with us to Russia. Unless of course you were willing to come alone . . . '

Tuesday shrank from the step and flung herself against her bear. 'No,' she breathed and Anushka nodded.

'Then you must learn to read and write, so we can

send for you if we find somewhere that would take both you and Promise.'

Tuesday swallowed hard. She wished she could fall into Anushka's arms and cry her heart out. 'Will you teach me to hunt?' she asked instead.

'Of course,' Anushka whispered in a voice as soft as a cloud.

As Tuesday and her beloved bear moved away from the welcoming wagon, back toward their own little cage, the winter felt colder than ever before.

Chapter 12

FALLING FROM GRACE

Four weeks later as the curtain closed on a show of ice and starlight, Tuesday smiled at her enthralled audience, her arm extended, her hand gripping Promise's paw, so she could steady him.

They had made it through another night. She sank into a gracious bow, genuinely relieved that the show was over. Every night Promise resisted the box a little more. Every night Tuesday tried to hide this from Gretta. Every night *North Star* inched a little nearer, a protective ring slowly closing around her.

Gretta didn't like it one bit and had banned both Tuesday and Promise from company mealtimes. Even though no one else objected, they were brought their supper in their wagon. But it was never enough, not really.

Once the audience had filed out, Tuesday led Promise

to the side of the stage and eased his skates off. She slipped out of her glorious white-gold costume and pulled on her lavender practice skirt, before changing her skates and helping Zarina pack the props away.

Promise eyed her darkly from the corner and she sighed. 'Alright boy. It's over for another night.' He tilted his snout in the direction of the little fire and food camp, which was being set up on the snow-kissed ice. Tuesday shook her head and moved toward him, taking his furry cheeks in her hands. 'No, my love. Let's go foraging instead,' she smiled.

As the moon glowed silver, Tuesday crossed the ice plains and stepped into a scarlet forest, Promise nuzzling her heels. She held a small torch with her, though her eyes were mostly accustomed to the dark. She crouched low to inspect mushrooms, peeled back chunks of moon-coloured bark, for Promise to chew on, or searched under clumps of bracken and snow for rare winter berries.

Tuesday had never been educated. Gretta said there was no time for it. She couldn't read, or tell the time, or understand anything beyond basic maths—though *North Star* were secretly helping her change this. But instead Tuesday had learned the ways of the woods and the different moods of the seasons.

She could tell the different types of snowfall by the way the flakes danced across her skin. She knew the fragments of the month by glancing at the Arctic moon. She could coax flame out of flint. Stitch a hide into the warmest winter mittens. Whittle a birch branch into a silver-cut arrow. But their hunting still needed practice.

They didn't speak as they moved through the trees. The girl and her bear. The child and her fearsome shadow. They didn't need to. For their language was so much more than words. It was the tread of their feet, the rhythm of their breath, falling and rising at different times, the knowledge of their beating hearts, that they would follow each other over the edge of the steepest valley, or up to the place where the river meets the sky.

Something scuffled in the undergrowth and both of them halted in a perfect stillness. Tuesday held out a gloved palm, motioning clearly for Promise to stay still, as she silently dropped to her knees. Ever so gently she eased a bow off her back and as quietly as she could manage, took a little wooden arrow from her coat pocket. She'd crafted the arrows herself and they were a little bit chunky and heavy.

In front of her the bushes began trembling as some small animal burrowed forward. Promise jerked his head up and gave a low growl. Tuesday frowned at him crossly. 'Quiet' she breathed, as she lined up her shot, hoping it was something old and slow. An injured hare who wanted peace. A bad rabbit who deserved to die. An ancient crow who was too old to fly. This was all

Tuesday could think of as she prepared to mortally wound the small thing in the leaves.

The rustling grew louder and louder and Tuesday found herself holding her breath, desperate to get the kill over. She made her heart as hard as ice. *Promise must eat, he must be strong.*

The dense leaves parted and a tiny black squirrel peered out, its little tail curling into an innocent question mark. Tuesday's fingers gripped her bow. She gritted her teeth. *Promise must live.* The squirrel looked at her quizzically, without any fear. It scampered forwar, its small nose twitching as it sniffed the night air. Tuesday closed her eyes and fired her shot, missing the squirrel completely and striking a nearby tree.

'Dammit!' Tuesday yelled, as in a flash of sleek fur the squirrel vanished and Promise galloped lazily after it.

She threw the bow down giving a howl of frustration. 'Why couldn't I just shoot it?' she huffed, driving her fists into the soft-packed snow. Promise plodded about in the bushes quietly chomping at frozen nettles. He didn't have the hunting instinct. Gretta had all but beaten it out of him, taught him that food came out of a barrel or a tin or off a metal plate. And he rarely had meat; it was normally something plant-based to discourage him from hunting altogether.

Tuesday rose, pulled the arrow out of the trees and

reached out to stroke Promise's back as he lumbered toward her. 'I'm sorry boy,' she sighed. 'It was a baby . . . it hadn't lived any life yet. I just couldn't do it.' Promise gave Tuesday such a look of disapproval that she burst out laughing. 'Next time, boy. Next time,' she said patting his head and turning back to the trees.

They had hardly taken a step forward when a noise stopped them. It was a high-pitched little moan, a helpless bleating. Tuesday frowned; there was something terribly familiar about it. 'Pro—' she began, but he had already begun strolling in the direction the sound was coming from. Tuesday took off at a sprint, darting in front of him, holding a hand up to signal 'stop'. Promise paused, lowering his head to nudge Tuesday forward. 'Alright, just go slowly,' she whispered as they moved on together.

Tuesday had seen him behave like this a few times before and it was always when an animal was injured. She bit her lip a little hoping it was something small that she could kill easily. *Maybe a rook or raven, some sort of bird.* The bleating came again and Tuesday winced. *Not a bird. An Arctic fox?* She hoped against hope it wasn't one of the dogs.

Then Tuesday froze as the woods seemed to part, for there in front of them in a clearing of long fallen leaves was Buttermilk the goat. The carnival's only goat, the one Lucie had named. Because she gave them butter and milk.

She was lying on her side, a trail of blood leaking from her throat, the same deep scarlet as the leaves, her dull eyes fluttering shut. Tuesday gave a little gasp and fell to her knees. Behind her Promise stopped, his breath heavy. Then he lurched forward at a speed that astonished Tuesday.

'No!' she cried, knowing it was already too late. The poor little goat was already dead.

Do wild polar bears even hunt goats? Tuesday wondered. Uncle Tolya had told her that they hunt seals and fish out on the ice—but goats? Jude had once said that the reason the audience gazed at Tuesday as if she was a girl made of stardust, was because bears like Promise were thought of as fatally dangerous. *But would a bear eat a goat? Yes if he was hungry. But this wasn't just any goat.*

A strangled gulp came from the other side of the clearing as Lucie and her brothers stepped through the midnight woods. Lucie's large eyes gazed mournfully at Promise, then the dead goat at his feet, the red blood upon his fur. Lovely Lucie, who was a year younger than Tuesday, who treated Buttermilk as a pet and had always been a little nervous of the great bear.

'Lucie, he didn't hurt her—we found her,' Tuesday said, trying to explain. But Lucie looked aghast, darting away, her tears scattering like leaves, the others running after her.

Tuesday sat down hard, the wind knocked from her lungs. *If Lucie thinks Promise killed Buttermilk . . . Poor Lucie . . .* Then her heart plunged to her toes. *What will happen to Promise?*

If the other members of North Star thought Promise was killing animals they wouldn't think it safe for Tuesday to live in a sled-wagon with him. They would try to separate her from her beloved bear. But he couldn't sleep without her. She couldn't breathe without him.

'Promise, come,' she gestured away from camp. Through the glimmering starlight his deep eyes found hers. 'Water,' she said, hoping there was some nearby. If she could clean him up, convince the adults he'd not harmed the goat they might just be OK. For now.

She fell in step beside him, running to the same rhythm of his paws, biting her lip. It was hard not to panic. Behind them came shouts and cries from the other performers anxiously calling her name. But Tuesday closed her ears to them. *Let me just get the blood out of his fur.*

At last they came to a small frozen stream. Tuesday hacked and smashed at the ice, working a chunk of it loose in her hands and letting the ice melt run over her bear, scrubbing at his snout and paws, determinedly.

Promise seemed to sense her dark mood and rolled into a sitting position in front of Tuesday. On the little frozen night river he leant his forehead into her chest, his eyes pressed closed, with a gesture that was so tender, there was no greater love in all the world. Tuesday wrapped her shivering arms around him and breathed in the scent of his wet fur. He smelled of melted snow and adventures.

A tall figure burst onto the riverbank calling her name. 'I'm here,' Tuesday answered, peering at the silhouette and realizing it was Sebastian, Lucie's father. He looked angry and troubled all at once. 'Tuesday! Thank goodness . . . What's going on?'

'We were out for a walk in the woods and we found Buttermilk . . .' she answered. 'Buttermilk was already dead—Promise didn't hurt her . . .' There was an eerie silence as Sebastian gazed at the girl on the river.

'Everybody knows how much you love that bear. Gretta has let you get too close to him, and after all he is just an animal.' Tuesday clutched her chest and shook her head. 'No one will blame you for this Tuesday, but you must tell the truth.'

'I am,' she said, as defiantly as she dared.

'Then why are you cleaning blood from his fur?' he asked, a lot more softly now.

Tuesday stood up straighter than any tree in the woods. 'Because I saw how upset Lucie was, and I knew you wouldn't believe me.'

She couldn't see it but in the thick night air Sebastian

sorrowfully smiled. *The girl has the courage of a bear herself* he thought.

'Let's get you both home,' he said, holding out a hand to Tuesday, but she scrambled out of the river on her own, Promise casually lumbering out behind her. They tramped back to camp in silence, the white bear between them. At the edge of the forest they stopped, abruptly, as a terrible row unfurled in front them.

'You've put too much weight on that girl's shoulders,' cried Anushka, her voice cracking with rage, as a sobbing Lucie clung to her legs.

Tuesday blinked through the starry dark in amazement. Anushka was a strong woman, but she rarely raised her voice to anyone. Let alone Gretta.

The old woman stood statue-still, her face unmoving, her grey hair turned ghostly white by the moonlight. 'Nonsense,' she snapped viciously.

'They've grown up together and anyone can see they adore each other,' Anushka said. 'But he's a wild animal. If he's killing goats, how do we know what he'll do next? How do we know it won't be her, or one of our children . . . ?'

'Because we will make sure,' said Gretta, her tone like ice. 'Promise will be suitably punished. He'll be made to understand.'

'Anything you do to the bear will only hurt the girl— you may as well rip out her heart,' hissed Anushka.

There was a tense pause.

'This will be our last season. We leave in the spring.' Anushka scooped up her trembling daughter and stalked away.

Gretta gave an exhausted sigh and sat down looking quite deflated on a tree stump. The wind whipped up the snow and there came the light crunch of footsteps as a concerned-looking Yusef approached. 'Did Promise hurt the goat?' asked Yusef.

Slowly Gretta shook her head. 'No. It was not the bear,' she said coldly. 'That child was getting too big for her boots, letting the bear get too close to everyone.'

Tuesday felt the ground shift, and the dark frozen leaves rushed up to meet her as she sank to the ground, catching a sob in her throat and swallowing it down. Promise laid his head on her lap and she gripped his two small ears. Beside them Sebastian put his hand over his mouth to stop himself from swearing.

'My god, the woman is a witch,' he muttered instead.

Gretta gave a cross sigh. 'I didn't expect Anushka to quit, but there are plenty of other acrobats around. I suppose we'll find more.'

Yusef gave a brisk nod. 'You did what you had to do,' he said in a simpering voice. 'We'll punish Promise however you think—'

'No,' growled Tuesday, and Sebastian moved around Promise, squatted beside her and put a warm arm around her shoulders.

Just for a moment Tuesday felt a tiny flicker of parental love, as if in that moment beneath those wild red trees she was his daughter too. Then he moved away from her, strolling into the moonlight and Tuesday shivered; her damp clothes were starting to freeze.

'You'll do nothing to the bear or the child,' said Sebastian calmly.

Yusef looked ashen, but Gretta rose to her feet completely composed. 'We will do whatever Yusef wants; it's his carnival.'

Sebastian held her gaze. 'Promise has done nothing wrong and everyone will know it.'

'Is that so?' said Gretta cruelly.

'It is,' Sebastian answered, walking away. He turned at the last moment just before he reached the camp, glancing over his shoulder. 'Like my wife said. We leave in the spring.' Then he was gone.

Tuesday didn't listen to Gretta and Yusef's fretful whispering. She pulled herself up, leant on her bear and staggered back to their wagon, looping away from them. 'We have to get out of here boy. We have to leave *North Star*,' she murmured as they got near. Promise snuffled her hair in agreement.

'I love this carnival,' Tuesday whispered, taking in the dogs with their boundless energy, the glorious colours of the wagons, the jokes and songs that passed between the people as they started to decamp. Lastly, her dark jewel-like eyes came to rest on the bars of their sled-wagon, the cage.

'But it's not our home,' she said, turning to Promise, their foreheads touching. He gave a soft whinny of a grunt and Tuesday hugged him. 'You're my whole world,' she breathed, drying her tears on his fur.

We'll wait for no one. We'll leave before the ice melts and find the island of bears.

Chapter 13

THE SNOWSTORM

No one heard anything more about *The Carnival of Northern Stars,* and winter on the island rolled by full of snowfall and hockey and watchful bears.

Though Marv never forgot. A lonesome girl and her bear still skated through his restless dreams, and sometimes he sat at the window gazing up at the all-seeing moon, wondering if Tuesday could see it too.

One night when the moon was at its peak, Marv was startled by an urgent knocking. He bounded down the stairs, flanked by Mya. Indi reached the door before them and threw it open to reveal Leon, back home early from the airport with Trucker, his eyebrows caked in icicles.

'Did you forget your key?' asked Indi indignantly, Leon shook his head.

'Last plane came in early, brought a special visitor.

Trucker's just dropping him home.'

'OK,' said Indi, peering blankly at the figure in the truck. 'Who is it?'

But Marv was pushing past them leaping through the snow in his slippers. Yanking the truck door open, light streamed out. 'How's it going Jackson?' came Florian's voice. Marv gave him the biggest grin, hopping in beside him.

'Do you want to come in, have a coffee?' called Indi.

'No I'm good thanks,' Florian replied, giving her a light salute.

Marv noticed the two crutches wedged beside Florian. The plaster on his knee.

'Are you hurt?'

'Yep, smashed up my knee. I'm most likely out for the season.' Marv caught the conflicted look on the hockey star's face and winced. 'But at least I get to train you guys.' Florian grinned, and suddenly the night didn't seem as dark, and the wind felt less glacial.

Florian had that easy way about him that made everything seem better.

Trucker climbed in and Marv turned, hugged Florian goodbye then darted back through the snow, running inside.

As the truck pulled away Marv watched from the window, thinking about the last time he'd seen Florian in Vancouver. Not long after he'd met Tuesday.

The girl who danced with a bear.

As he watched the truck lurch roughly up the hill, a pale shadow caught his eye. It had a silvery quality like a starlit cloud. Marv peered hard, his heartbeat picking up as he realized it was a bear, just well hidden, at the tree line on the other side of the Raven.

Her eyes found his and Marv gave a mild gasp. It was his bear. There she was silently watching and waiting.

For what?

For me?

Again Marv got the swift sense that she wanted him to follow her, and he wished with all his heart that he could. But it was impossible ever to trust a bear; he had the very scar that proved this.

He reached up and touched his moon-mark, swiftly remembering Tuesday's silvered arms.

But she trusts her bear. It's as if their souls are one, like one of those Nevkian myths.

He drifted to sleep, and stories of Ice Daughters haunted his dreams.

🌲 🌲 🌲

A week later the school was shut due to snowfall. Marv and Mya were supposed to be completing work from home, when the doorbell chimed brightly through the house. 'I'm on the phone, can one of you get that?' called Indi, who was working in the study.

'I'll go!' both brother and sister yelled, wrestling to get to the door first.

Mya won, opening the door to Rae and the darker-than-night dog, Eden. Marv pushed past his sister and stroked the dog's black, frost-covered ears. 'She likes you,' Rae said.

'She's a great dog,' Marv agreed.

Rae stared at him with the calmness that comes from living in forests. 'She's not exactly a dog, and she's not really mine. She's of the island.'

'Whatever, can we, like, just close the door already! I'm freezing,' snapped Mya.

They left Eden outside to slink away of her own accord and crowded into the living room. Rae stamped the snow off her boots and peeled off her snowsuit, then signalled for them to close the door.

'I think I found the carnival,' she whispered, pulling a rolled-up map from her sleeve.

'What?' Marv half yelled, as he and Mya both stared at the map in amazement. 'Where—how? We have to go!'

'Last night my Dad got in real late—which isn't unusual, but then he called Coach.' Mya and Marv both glanced at each other—this wasn't out of the ordinary as all the older islanders were the core of a tight-knit community. 'Then Coach came over, in the middle of a snowstorm, and they had coffee.'

'Yeah, and so?' Marv garbled, starting to feel exasperated.

'And I overheard my dad tell Coach that while he was driving home, he cut across the sea ice, and near one of the islets on the brink of Hudson Bay he saw an encampment of colourful wagons, positioned around a stage of black ice, lit by floodlights, welcoming in an audience.'

'That's them! That's it!' Marv shot to his feet.

'Coach said he'd speak to Polar Patrol, see what they could do,' went on Rae.

Marv frowned deeply. 'Why would they need Polar Patrol?'

'Well if they don't agree with what the carnival are doing, maybe they're going to try and get the girl out, re-wild the bear or give it to a zoo or something,' said Mya carefully.

Marv pushed his hands through his hair, knocking his cap off. He thought of Tuesday melting into the fur of her bear, the way they were so connected, the way the bear listened only to her, and he sat down hard on the couch. 'No . . . That's . . . They can't! What if she doesn't want to leave the carnival? What if she's happy? They can't just take the bear!'

Rae stared at him for a long while, then gingerly pushed the map into his hands. 'I guess you could warn her.'

Mya gaped at Rae in disbelief. 'Are you crazy? We can't! Look at the weather.'

Marv fiddled impatiently with his cap. 'But how long before the carnival leaves?'

Rae sat stock still. 'Not long,' she said at last.

The lounge door flew open and everyone jumped in shock. 'Guys . . . what's going on?' Indi asked, as they gazed at her with guilty expressions.

'Nothing much,' said Mya quickly. 'Just, um, some geography . . .'

'I'm going to take your father some tea at the airport. Nothing can fly in this snow. Will you kids be alright till I get back?'

The little group nodded at Indi as innocently as they could manage. As soon as she was gone Mya pored over the map. 'It's too far Marv. You could never skate there, it's just too dangerous.' There came a low, soulful moan.

Mya stared out of the window in disbelief. 'Marv she's here. Your bear. She's outside.' Then all three of them were squeezed up against the glass, and though it was misted with cold, and eager breath, and the world outside was crystal white, there was no denying the immense form of Marv's bear.

Marv rubbed the glass clear with his sleeve and the bear's eyes reached him. They were deep and searching, the colour of the forest at midnight. Her gaze seemed to extend beyond the snow, beyond the window, beyond all logic, and tug at him, asking him to step outside into the thickening dark.

'I'm going outside,' said Marv decisively.

'No way in hell,' said Mya firmly, but then she looked at her brother's face, and the beautiful moon-mark scar and his pleading frown and hopeful eyes, and turned away unable to break his heart further. 'We can't just go out after a bear,' she said quietly. 'Polar Patrol will be all over us, and mum would murder us.'

'Polar Patrol only gets involved if the bear's aggressive,' Rae reminded them. 'There are three of us and we'd keep our distance. We could take skates. And if we really need it I've got my dad's stun gun. One dart and it would send a bear to sleep for an hour or so.' Marv and Mya both nearly fell over at this. 'It's just a small one; it fits in my bag. I always carry it during bear season . . . I live in the forest . . . '

'Have you ever used it?' asked Mya, wide-eyed.

Rae shook her head. 'Never. But I know how to.'

Outside the bear growled tenderly. Across the lounge Mya met her brother's brown eyes, like her own but with less green in them. But she shook her head. 'We can't Marv. It's not safe.'

'OK, how about we go first thing tomorrow instead?' suggested Rae. 'Polar Patrol won't leave the island in this weather. I doubt the carnival would get far either.' And even though it pained Marv to the core he agreed.

Time ticked by, and after they'd planned the route they would take, and Rae had called her mom to say she was staying at the Jacksons', the girls went upstairs to watch a movie.

But Marv could not keep still. After what felt like an eternity he moved to the front door, and opened it ajar.

Fractured moonlight rushed in around him. The streets were already aglow with lamplight, the glitter of ice formations hanging from rooftops catching the distant dazzle of stars.

The island seemed empty. His bear had gone. Marv closed the door and stepped back. And then he found himself lacing up his skates, adjusting his hockey helmet, securing his gloves. He glanced at Rae's backpack, remembering what she'd said about the stun gun, and reluctantly pushed the map into it and slipped the bag over his shoulders.

He crept cautiously through the back door, taking a stick from the shed to light later on, and a torch, and his phone, though he doubted there'd be any reception in the middle of the sea.

Then with his heart in his throat, he stumbled out of the back yard and clambered onto the River Raven, racing downhill toward the town and the sea, his skates slicing through the snow like knives through icing.

Marv expected people to come out of their houses and question him. Or his parents to drive home early. Or a bear to suddenly bolt after him. But none of these things happened; instead a flurry of feather-soft flakes descended over the island, whitening window panes and covering his tracks. Soon the smooth white beach was in sight and Marv tumbled off the river and stomped clumsily toward frost-sprinkled sand. He was half blinded by the bite of snow, deafened by the roar of the wind, yet the urgency to find the carnival carried him toward the sea ice.

It was hard to tell where the earth became ice, as everything was coloured by night. But as Marv's blades began to move smoothly over the silken sea, he relaxed. He paused just once, stopping quickly to check the co-ordinates of the map and light the torch, glancing all around as he did. The whole island looked deserted apart from the twinkle of lights and the far-off glint of the rink. Marv blocked out the sound of the wind, the voice of his own guilt for not telling his sister that he was going, and the agonizing worry he would cause his parents, and skated out across the frozen sea.

He had not travelled more than three glides when a moonlit shape emerged from the Arctic air. Marv screeched to a stop, digging his blades firmly into the ice.

His heart seemed to beat against his very bones.

A bear.

Marv thrust the lit torch up high above him.

The bear grizzled knowingly. Marv stood very still, staring at her through the bars of his helmet, trying not to tremble. And he knew who she was. Last time they had met like this he had been five. She had been a mother protecting her cub.

The great bear turned a docile head toward him, her slow-blinking eyes finding his, and Marv realized how measured her movements were, how old she must be. How tired and weak she seemed. No longer the fearsome mother bear who gave him his scar, but a wiser, sombre beast, almost at the end of her life. She looked like she wanted to lie down.

Shadows and storm clouds blotted out the moon. The snow fell thick and fast and wonderful, and the bear turned her snout away from the island. Marv took the deepest breath he had ever taken in all his life, counted quietly to three, then skated hard, sailing effortlessly past her. He heard the soft crunch of paws as the bear began to follow, running at a gentle pace over the ice. She moved slowly for a bear, but it was still fast.

All the hours of training at the rink, all the years of skating on Lake Rarity, all the games he'd all but broken bones to win, every time he'd laced his skates up, it all seemed to have been leading to this moment.

The night he led a bear to a carnival in the middle of the frozen sea.

The muscles in Marv's legs burned as he fought against the force of the wind. His bones shuddered and jolted every time his blade hit a lump in the ice. But he thought of Florian, always moving forward, always searching out the puck, always thinking ahead, darting around his opponents on ballet-light toes and he pushed on.

Soon he could barely feel his feet, or his fingers or cheek bones, and the rest of his body was drenched in sweat. Beside him his bear was pacing through the snow, seeming as tired as him.

He didn't stop to think about whether he'd live or die; he ploughed through a snowstorm, neck and neck with his bear, until it seemed that rest of his whole young life would be spent skating, like this journey would never end. And at that very moment he saw the twinkle of spotlights and his heart surged with joy.

He crashed to his knees on the ice, clutching his side where a stitch was paining him, the fire-stick hissing to smoke in the snow. The bear stilled beside him. Marv raised the cage of his helmet so he could breathe, and the wind could dry his dripping hair. The bear growled, a low raw sound, and Marv nearly died of fear.

He struggled to his feet, ignoring the shooting pain that was travelling up one leg, and made himself face her. The snow beast stared at him intently and Marv's heart hammered wildly. Was this it? Would she turn on him again? Punish him for her missing cub? But the bear gave a snort and stumbled on towards the carnival.

Chapter 14

RACING THE MOON

Inside *The Carnival of Northern Stars* the curtain was falling across a stage of black ice where a young girl dressed as a doll, took a bow with her beloved bear. The applauding audience were moved beyond their wildest imaginings.

Tuesday smiled her brightest smile, a carefully practised smile used just for the stage, relief flooding through her. No one but Jude knew the immense effort it had taken for her to convince Promise to climb back in the wretched box.

Again.

Uncle Tolya had cut a huge escape hole into the back of it, so they could at least both see out. Both breathe. But still it took Tuesday every ounce of patience and courage to perform this routine every night. And moments before the opening of the show the same nervous thoughts whirred through her mind.

How much longer will Promise do this? Not long . . . Please hold on until I get us out of here.

As the spotlight found her for her final bow she glanced up, pushing her untamed curls from her brow, her eyes darting over each unfamiliar face, as if she were searching for someone or something. But none of them had brown eyes, with the tiniest fleck of green or scar from a bear that glinted on their cheek. None of them were Marvel.

Tuesday had not stopped thinking about that boy, that scar, that island.

As winter wore on, the snow showed no signs of lifting, the sea still a frozen landscape enchanted by ice. But the dawn was already coming earlier, the sunshine a little brighter. And at the back of Tuesday's mind the promise she had made herself burnt like a flame that would not go out.

We'll wait for no one. We'll leave before the ice melts and find the Isle of Bears.

She had, with Jude's help, located Marvel's hometown on a map, which they had had to borrow from Uncle Toyla's ancient Arctic atlas, hoping he wouldn't notice the torn out page.

The very same crinkled page that was carefully folded in Tuesday's hand-stitched bag at the side of the stage.

The curtains had closed and the cheering faded.

Tuesday knelt down and unfastened Promise's huge skates, tugging them quickly off his feet. He might never wear them again . . . The thought felt so sad to Tuesday; she loved skating with her bear. But she didn't have time to return to the sled-wagon, and leaving the skates discarded by the stage felt wrong to her. She glanced about and slipped them into her large rabbit fur bag, next to the map. Hans and Franco began wearily to pack up the props, while Zarina folded away the costumes.

'I'll leave mine on if that's OK—there are just a few jumps I need to quickly rehearse,' she smiled, hating herself for lying.

This cape is the warmest thing I own she reminded herself. And she pulled it firmly around her, led Promise to the back of the stage, and began diligently marking the steps to one of their routines.

In the month since Buttermilk had died, the acrobat family had ignored Gretta's rules, overstepping invisible boundaries to include Tuesday more. Jude and Zarina, too, had drawn secretly closer to her. Teaching her more about the world, educating her about the places they had visited, showing her drawings of the wider world, so she knew geography not just from the landscape, but from charting the stars and reading a compass.

On the coldest evenings Zarina had come to sit with Tuesday, under the guise of mending costumes, and covertly taught her how to cook over firewood. How to use dried berries and spices to flavour food so that a simple mushroom soup became a delicious hearty broth. Or how a skinned rabbit could be divided into many different dishes, including the bone.

Sebastian had come out with her when Gretta and Yusef were distracted and taught her how to hunt. How to spear an animal through the eye with a finely whittled arrow. She never hesitated any more. She had even killed and skinned a black squirrel, and learned how to crack the ice and catch glorious fresh fish. To Tuesday's delight, Sebastian even tried teaching Promise to hunt, not that he was any good at it.

And in her heart Tuesday knew she was ready. 'All we need is a snowstorm,' she had told herself, night after night. And now—tonight—a blizzard was here.

Jude was the only person who knew of her plan, and right this moment he was on his way to 'accidentally' set two of the dogs free. Gretta loved those dogs like she loved the ice; there was no way she would let them go without a fight.

Tuesday put all of her skittering energy into her skating, leaping and jumping furiously around a slightly befuddled Promise.

There came a keening yip of freedom and Tuesday's breath caught in her throat as she waited for the frantic patter of husky paws. There it was—the dogs were running wild. Tuesday peered around wide-eyed trying to look as confused as everyone else. A furious bellowing rent the air as Gretta shouted out in panic. All around Tuesday the stage emptied as the rest of *North Star* ran to help. Tuesday steadied her breath. Counted to ten on her gloved fingers, giving everyone time to begin chasing the dogs. A flurry of snowflakes seemed to whirl in her tummy, and she bit down on a tendril of hair to calm her nerves. Her bear gazed at her quizzically. 'It's OK, my darling,' Tuesday mouthed, gently laying one hand on Promise's snowy fleece; with the other she pointed firmly in the direction of the ice plains, clearly as if she were commanding the stars. The fur along Promise's back rose as he sensed Tuesday's intention. She gave him a rare hopeful smile and whispered, 'Run.'

And Promise fled, nose raised to the sky, as if in defiance of his years in the carnival, galloping lightly on his four huge feet. Tuesday gave a small gasp of joy and flew across the ice beside him, skating as if her heart were on fire. Over the black ice, past the fire-lit audience tent, onto the moon-kissed frozen sea they rushed.

Tuesday did not look back. She didn't dare. She raced toward her future. And as the lights of the carnival dimmed behind them and their tracks were hidden by the snow, Tuesday couldn't keep from smiling.

Marv's bear was running steadily in front of him now,

and he was glad of her company. No one would notice him approach the carnival if he kept behind his regal ice beast. *As long as they don't hurt her* he thought darkly, remembering the poker. A snowflake settled on his scar and another bleaker thought crossed his mind.

As long as she doesn't hurt them.

A sharp gust of wind tore the clouds apart and tossed the snow up like blossom. Moonlight glanced off the ice, bathing the world in warm glow. Marv squinted at the horizon. *Is that a girl in a long cloak? And a bear . . .*

He was freezing anyway, but his blood turned colder. *Was he witnessing a myth? Was this a Nevkian, come to save him, or fight him?*

He pushed up the bars of his helmet and squinted hard, giving a sharp gasp. The sight of them almost knocked him down. For there was no mistaking the graceful rushing glory of Tuesday's skating. And the handsome bounding bear beside her could only be Promise.

Marv's bear gave an anguished growl. Marv's bones turned to ice as he remembered his dream: The storm. The girl dancing beneath a sweeping night sky. The roar of the mama bear splitting the sky in two.

What would happen if his bear found Tuesday before he did . . . ? Marv bent low, running toward Tuesday with every gasp of breath he had. Up ahead, the two bears charged toward each other.

A sound cut through the storm. 'Tuesday!' She whirled around in panic, wondering if Yusef had followed her after all. But there was nothing. Was the cruel wind playing tricks on her, crying her name?

Tuesday slowed her skating ever so slightly, shielding her eyes to peer through the moonlit dark. At first all she saw was a figure in a hockey helmet speeding toward her.

'Get back!' he yelled. 'There's a—' But Tuesday didn't hear the end because Promise gave a sudden single growl. An answering howl came on the wind and a shape cut from cloud and claw loomed in front of them. Tuesday skidded to a dramatic halt as a huge bear ran through the moonlight.

Then her heart was in her throat. 'Promise, stop!' she screamed.

He doesn't know how to fight a bear . . . He'll get hurt.

The moon burned the ice and Tuesday swept in front of Promise, a sharply whittled arrow raised to a bow at her shoulder.

The mama bear picked up speed. Tuesday stood frozen, the arrow aimed perfectly.

'Stop!' Marv shouted, and hoping against hope that he was right and the mama bear meant no harm he dived, flying across the ice, cutting across the path of the bear and taking Tuesday down.

The arrow clattered to a stop on the ice, the two

skaters slid out of the bear's path, spinning like snow angels, as the mama and her grown cub faced each other beneath the luminous sky.

They bounded around each other like two frantic dogs. Then they slowed in the snowfall. The mama bear gave a soft grizzle. Promise stared for a long moment then began circling her, until they met in stillness, their two snouts touching.

Tuesday gave a cry of relief, wiping sweat and sleet from her eyes. Marv coughed hard, spitting out a mouthful of churned up snow, rubbing his scraped elbow and grazed chin.

'Marvel,' Tuesday spluttered, slowly sitting up, shaking snow out of her hair, 'what are they doing?'

'I think they are saying hello,' Marv replied.

Tuesday was wrapped in her snow leopard cloak, her bow and arrows and bag slung across her back, rabbit fur mittens on her hands and a look of determination on her face, so sharp it could almost cut you.

'I can't believe we found you both,' Marv breathed.

Tuesday rose to her feet graceful as a swan, ever the ice ballerina. 'No . . . we found you,' she said, a smile creeping into her voice.

'What are you doing out here on your own?' asked Marv suddenly bewildered.

'I'm running away from the carnival. We can't stay there any more. I was going to find your island.'

Marv blinked in amazement.

'I can take you there,' he said, stumbling uneasily to his feet.

'Will Promise be safe there?'

Marv didn't know how to answer. He thought of Rae's words. *Polar Patrol only gets involved if a bear's aggressive.*

'He won't be in any danger, as long as he's with you, I guess,' he said gently. 'And we can explain who he is.'

'Promise, come.' The order was clear as a winter's bell. For a heartbeat the bear seemed not to hear her, then he turned his head and his eyes found hers and he trotted obediently to her, nuzzling her hair with his nose. Tuesday wrapped her arms tightly around his neck. 'You're my whole world,' she breathed.

She stared at the other bear. The great graceful white beast was as wild as the storm itself. And for one heart-splitting moment she wondered if Promise would be happier out here with his own kind, on the ice sheets.

He can't hunt came her tumbling thoughts.

He has no fear of humans, she realized, imagining the danger this would put him in.

He's not wild, she thought, feeling both sorrow for her bear and huge relief at not having to do the unthinkable and say goodbye.

'Who is this bear—is she yours?'

Marv chuckled and shook his head. 'No. Not at all.

She's the bear who gave me my scar . . . a long time ago. I think she might be Promise's mother.'

Tuesday became very still. She laid a hand on Promise and together they moved over the ice to the mama bear.

Marv felt a claw of worry scrape his heart. But he held back. At a safe distance Tuesday paused, she stared at the bear, into eyes the colour of the forest at midnight, and she knew. She just knew, this bear was Promise's mama.

'Ready?' asked Marv.

She glanced at him, her eyes deep and serious. 'Ready.'

Moonlight glittered darkly on the ice. Snowflakes chased each other across the night in little whirls. The wind whispered around them chanting its ghostly lullaby. For a moment they faced each other, two children, on the brink of the world, the brink of a storm, the brink of a thousand possibilities, then they skated side by side out into the star-struck dark, toward the Isle of Bears.

Marv had expected the mother bear to follow, or protest, or show some feral opinion. But instead she stood in a dazzle of starlight, her snout tipped to the sky, and she sang. Both Tuesday and Marv whipped around on their skates so they were flying backwards, entranced by her cry. It was not the sad, haunting howl of Marv's birthdays. It was uplifting, a soft calling farewell.

Marv wiped his eyes on his gloves, feeling as if he

was saying goodbye. As if this was the last time he would see her.

Seeming to sense him, the bear cocked her head, her slow unblinking eyes meeting his, then staring past Marv at Promise. Promise paused, locked eyes with his mama and echoed her song, singing to the moon. Tuesday leaned into her bear, voice ringing out meeting his. Marv felt as if the world was suddenly magical.

Then their song ceased and the mama bear sat down in the snow. Promise nuzzled Tuesday's hair and together they both turned away.

Marv span back around, took Tuesday's hand, and they flung themselves forward, Promise racing a little way ahead.

The wind was strangely calm and all Marv could hear was the gasp of their breath and rolling plod of the bear. *Her bear.*

But if the wind was soft, the snow was relentless. It stuck to their blades, making them leap and bounce. Marv was amazed to notice Tuesday hardly fell; she would stumble then catch herself in a breathtaking jump. Tuesday was quietly astonished by how fast Marv could skate; even when he crashed to the ice, he shot back up and staggered on.

After a little while, Marv paused, peering hard through the ceaseless snow. 'I can't see the island,' he shouted, kneeling down, pulling out Rae's map and using the light from his phone to try and read it. It was useless. The snow soaked everything, the wind ripping the map from his hands.

The far-off glittering land mass should have been in sight by now. Even in the thickest snowfall you could normally always see its lone lighthouse, spilling its glow over the ice like the star of the north. Only now there was nothing but merciless black sky and blinding snow.

Are we going the right way? Marv wondered. *Are we lost?*

Tuesday moved closer to Marv, and Promise leant his huge body into them, shielding them as best he could from the storm. Apart from the night of the attack Marv had never been this close to a bear, never felt its rough breath upon his neck. He was shivering hard, his teeth relentlessly chattering, his bones aching desperately. Tuesday dropped to her knees and pulled a fine-spun pink shawl from her bag, tucking it closely around Marv's neck and shoulders. He was beginning to convulse with the cold, the dried sweat beneath his clothes turning icy.

'We've got to keep moving,' she said gently, and to Marv's amazement he noticed she wasn't shaking at all. She was serene, a maiden made of moonlight, untouched by the blizzard.

Is she magical? Marv thought in his half delusional state. And he wondered if her bones were carved from ice, her soul paired with her bear's, her heart beating for the ceaseless snow.

Tuesday took a compass out of the pocket of her cape and consulted the sky, then glanced at the map. 'It's this way,' she said, determinedly.

Marv wasn't sure, he felt so tired, but also very awake, as if nothing was real any more, like he had skated into a world of his own imaginings.

'Marvel, stand!' Her voice was urgent, an icicle cutting through mist, and Marv knew he had to obey her. To stay still would be the death of them. Tuesday held her hand out to him and pulled him to his feet. Dizziness made him nauseous, but the years of being knocked through hockey games gave him the strength to push through it. Tuesday leant into him, slipping an arm around his wais, and together they skated on, wobbling and cursing and picking their way over the ice.

They hadn't travelled very far when the slice and scrape of skates reached their ears. Tuesday froze, churning up snow in a T-stop, throwing her arms around Promise to still him, a bow and arrow flying into her hands.

'It's alright,' said Marv, as a figure came careering toward them at the speed of light. He was grace and energy all in one, with no sign of a knee injury.

'Jackson! What in the name of—' Florian came up

sharp, as he took in the child and the bear. He leant backwards grinding to a halt. He had grown up with the sovereigns of winter ever in his periphery, but in all his twenty-seven years he had never been this close to a wild bear.

'This is Tuesday,' Marv began, putting a hand on her shoulder. 'Tuesday, this is Florian. He's from the Isle of Bears. He's a friend.'

'Marv, your family are going insane with worry. Trucker and your dad are back there in the truck, but the snow was too deep, so I skated ahead. What the hell is—'

Marv suddenly skated into his arms, found his honey-coloured eyes. 'I think Tuesday is from the island,' he said, gripping Florian's shoulders. 'We have to bring her home.'

Florian stood with folded arms trying to weigh up what to do. Marv was like a little brother to him. And he found himself listening, believing every word the boy said. Tuesday gazed about nervously, as if she was desperate to flee. Florian murmured a quiet curse and found himself saying, 'Nice to meet you, miss.'

'Nice to meet you too,' she said very solemnly, the bear moving nearer, nestling his nose into her hood.

And something about the undying pride of her almost knocked Florian off balance. The look that settled upon her brow—it was familiar to him. He couldn't place it, but she reminded him of thunder and sunlight knitted together. He took a snowbound breath.

'The truck's that way. You all better follow me.' And he turned on his blades and flew into the dark.

Behind him skated the boy, the girl, and the dancing bear. All of them so focused on racing forward they didn't hear the howl of sleigh dogs behind them.

Chapter 15

TO SLEEP BENEATH THE STARS

On they skated through the relentless northern dark, never looking back. Snow blinded them, but they closed their eyes to the white fury and raced on. Marv could not feel his face. Florian was numb apart from the ache in his knee, and Tuesday had never felt so out of breath, or so full of life. Whenever Tuesday or Marv tripped or stumbled, Florian was somehow there to steady them, years of hockey making him vividly aware of his little winter's night team.

A thick solid shape loomed in front of them. 'That's the truck!' Marv half yelled, trying to gesture to Tuesday.

'Leon, Trucker, it's us. I've got Marvel, a girl, and a PEACEFUL bear,' cried Florian through cupped hands.

Tuesday dug her blades into the snow, screeching to stillness, suddenly worried Promise might be too much of a shock for them. She darted in front of her bear and stood like an angel with her arms open to the sky.

Leon tumbled from the truck and crashed toward his son, stopping short at the sight of Tuesday, his hand covering his mouth in astonishment.

Trucker stepped down into the snow, moving with that slow, unperturbed manner the older islanders had, a lit rolled cigarette hanging from his lip. 'Who you got here, Marvel?'

Marv opened his mouth to speak, but her voice chimed through the storm, clear as starlight.

'My name is Tuesday. This is my brother, Promise.'

Trucker put his cigarette out in the snow. 'Won't your family, this carnival, be worried about you?'

'They're not my family,' said Tuesday with the same authority she used to direct Promise. 'And we were leaving them anyway.'

Snowflakes whirled and glittered beneath the stars, but Marv suddenly had the sensation of being watched.

Is it my bear? Has she come back?

He wheeled round as the growl of dogs cut through the snow, and a sleigh carrying a single statuesque passenger came hurtling over the frozen sea.

Her grey hair flew out behind her, catching the moonlight like the locks of a ghost. Her wolfskin kimono made her seem more wilderness than human. She was the Snow Queen, the White Witch, the woman who had done the impossible. Created an act like never before, trained a child to skate with a bear. She was not about to let them go.

A flurry of sleet stung everyone's eyes, but Gretta was untouched, a woman born for winters. Leon moved protectively toward his son and the girl, aware for the first time of how young Tuesday was despite her height. Trucker stood firm, the snow piling up around the wheels of the truck. They didn't have long before it would be too deep to drive in. Florian carefully put his weight on one skate, ignoring the pulsing in his knee.

'Moonrise Tuesday, what sort of mischief are you getting up to now?' Gretta laughed, and her voice was silvery sweet. Terrifying. The clever, crisp voice of a snow-witch.

Beneath her cape Tuesday started quivering, but she faced the old woman with an immovable stillness. Marv and Florian both instinctively drew closer to her. Trucker and Leon stepped forward and Promise gave such a vicious growl that everyone but Tuesday flinched.

'What can we do for you, ma'am?' asked Trucker carefully.

'That's my precious granddaughter. She must have got lost in the snow again. She thinks she's immortal because of her stupid, beautiful bear.' The old woman chuckled.

'Is that so?' Trucker answered, squinting at her through the dark with his piercing blue eyes.

'Now come along Tuesday, enough of this silliness. We need to get back and fetch Promise his tea. You know he can't hunt for himself; you don't want him going hungry do you?' For a moment nobody moved.

Tuesday felt trapped, sickened, chained to the carnival by Gretta's voice. For it was the voice of her childhood. The voice that had taught her to skate, sung her nursery rhymes, whispered her fairy tales.

Tuesday began to shake with the effort not to cry, but she forced her words out through the merciless cold. 'No. You're not my grandmother. We don't belong to you.'

'I am the only family you have!' said the old woman, spitefully. Promise very faintly began to growl.

'You're exploiting this child and the bear for entertainment,' Leon said, and Marv heard the quiet anger in his father's voice.

'I wouldn't expect you to understand the skill and grit needed to make such a miraculous act possible. But I can assure you, no laws have been broken and no one has been exploited. Tuesday and Promise live to skate together. And that bear—is mine. He belongs in the carnival. Now I really do have to get going,' she said, producing a huge rope from the sleigh and lassoing it perfectly over Promise's head in one fluid movement.

'No!' screamed Tuesday as the rope tightened around Promise's snowy neck, her small fingers fighting to loosen it.

Marv tried to help her, a swift gust of wind catching at his scarf, making it flutter. It was soft shell-pink, like a baby's blanket . . .

Then his heart was thumping in his ears.

'Where did you get the bear from?' he asked suddenly.

'That's not your concern,' Gretta snapped irritably.

'And where is Tuesday from?' he asked coolly.

'The carnival,' Gretta growled.

'But she's not your blood. She doesn't look like anyone else in the company,' Leon said. 'Where did you find her?'

'She was abandoned on the ice. Left to die. And I rescued her. And that ungrateful bear. His kind are dying out. But he's been kept warm and safe and not faced starvation. He lives like a king.'

Then Marv began speaking very quickly, the words tumbling out of him, fast and fierce.

'You found them both on the River Raven, on Tuesday the 7th of November. Tuesday was in a basket. She had one boot on and this blanket,' Marv gulped, holding up the scarf. 'Promise was beside her, an innocent cub, and you stole them together.'

Gretta paled a little and Tuesday went rigid.

'I saved her life,' said Gretta calmly.

There was a sharp intake of breath. Florian put his head in his hands in disbelief and Trucker turned to stare at Marv, his eyes sapphire-bright in the snow.

'My God,' Leon scrubbed at his face, 'There was a baby . . . son, I'm so sorry.'

Marv could hardly hear over his chattering teeth. He turned to Tuesday, trying to smile.

'You're from the Isle of Bears. You and Promise.' And he held the blanket out to her. 'Welcome home.'

Tuesday felt as if she was spinning, falling down a very dark hole. A sob caught in her throat.

'I rescued her,' Gretta bellowed, her grip tightening on the rope as she tried to drag Promise toward her by force. 'I gave you a purpose. A home. A family. I fed and clothed you.' Promise leaned away from her, wailing as the rope pulled taut. 'I trained you to be an incomparable ice dancer. Allowed you to live a dream. You will both come home with me at once!'

Trucker crunched over the deepening snow, putting himself between Gretta and Promise. 'You raised a bear, with no muzzle or harness,' he said respectfully. 'That's some skill you must have . . . But you took a child from her own community. It's time for her to come home now.'

The old woman leapt wolf-fast out of the sleigh, a huge knife in her gloved hand. 'Tuesday, you know how good at throwing knives I am,' she said, stalking toward them, the rope still coiled in one hand as she held the bear in place.

'Please don't hurt him,' Tuesday whimpered.

'If you do not get into the sleigh right this instant, I will throw this blade into that wretched bear's heart.'

'Don't do it!' cried Marv in desperation, and even though Tuesday was terrified, his words somehow reached her. She whirled in front of Promise, rooting her skates to the spot, tears streaming down her face as she opened her arms into the shape of a cross. Over her shoulder Promise stood on his hind legs, and roared. Gretta took aim. Trucker strode toward her, arms outstretched in peace, but she drew back her hand to throw the blade over him. Everyone moved at once, when a sound like mountains shattering rocked the world and something born of rage came pounding across the snow. Gretta hesitated, stepped back, then in panic threw the knife.

But not at Tuesday and Promise. At the ferocious mama bear that was charging toward her.

'Tuesday help! Get it to stop!' she screeched, as the bear opened her winter jaws.

Marv gasped in shock.

My bear, she must have followed us all along.

Tuesday let go of Promise and shot toward Gretta, trying to protect her. Florian caught Tuesday around the waist and held with all his strength. Even though she kicked him hard, cutting his legs through his weatherproof trousers, he didn't let go.

The knife struck Marv's bear through the heart as she howled hatefully into Gretta's face, swiping her to the ice with a paw, where Gretta lay groaning, a deep gash across her cheek. Trucker went to her side and slowly gathered her up and sat her in the sleigh.

A crimson stain seeped onto the mama bear's fur. She stood for a long moment then she turned to Promise, her eyes soft as she padded forward, before collapsing onto the ice.

Tuesday and Marv struggled to get the rope off Promise's neck and the great bear rushed to meet the fallen queen, their noses touching, a stillness falling over everyone as the snowflakes finally settled. There, beneath the light of the acorn moon, a mother kissed her son and closed her eyes to the waking world. Promise lowered his great mournful head and gave a low searing cry.

Tuesday dropped to her knees weeping. Marv tried to comfort her, though he found was softly sobbing. His bear had been such a huge part of his story. She was his worst and most loved memory.

Leon embraced both children in a hug and helped them stand, so together they could shuffle to Promise's side. The three of them huddled together against the elements. For the first time since the night of his scar

Marv knew for sure that Tuesday wasn't just a dream. The baby on the ice was real.

She is here.

'You're from the island, Tuesday,' he breathed. 'You're coming home.'

A thousand questions fluttered around Tuesday's mind, but she had no strength left to ask; all she could do was give a small grateful smile.

'No!' came a low guttural snarl. Gretta was on her feet. Swaying slightly, blood running down her cheek.

Trucker caught her as a terrible shriek escaped her throat. He spoke calmly as if he were dealing with a wild dog.

'Tuesday is coming home with us. Back to her island, and there's nothing to be done about it.' And he lifted Gretta onto the sleigh as she fought weakly against him, her strength knocked from her by the fall.

'They will never survive beyond the carnival. You wait and see,' Gretta spat furiously, before she shouted at the dogs in Russian, and went soaring away into the night.

Leon and Florian both knelt beside Marv and Tuesday, making a ring around them with their arms. Leaving a small space for Promise to be part of it.

Trucker moved to the mama bear and carefully drew back the knife. With a gentle hand he closed her eyes, then they all moved around her, covering her gently with snow, until she was at one with the wilderness again.

Marv kissed his gloved hand and laid it on her cold white cheek. Tuesday whispered a little winter's prayer and Promise nuzzled her farewell.

'We need to get going. Everyone into the truck!' cried Florian, swiftly glancing at the sky. Marv was shivering again violently, the sweat drying on his skin, and Tuesday was shaking with adrenalin. The tarpaulin of the truck at least kept the snow out.

Trucker assessed the wheels with an anxious frown, fetched a small trowel and began digging the truck out. Noticing this, Tuesday followed.

'Promise can help,' she said, pointing at the wheels and saying 'dig' with a sharp clarity. Promise bounded over and began burrowing away, clearing the snow with his paws.

'The bear does everything she asks.' Florian blinked in bewildered amazement. His family were all Polar Patrol—he'd grown up knowing only the wild northern temperament of these predators. He had never seen anything quite like this before.

Leon nodded. 'She's the real Ice Bear Miracle.'

Trucker started the engine, but it spluttered and choked. Everyone held their breath. He tried again, and the truck hissed to life, but the wheels only span uselessly in the snow. Tuesday whispered to her bear, and Promise stood like the king of winter and leant his weight against the back of the truck, pushing it forward up and over the snow.

At first it stuck. Then with a lurch it came free and lurched forward startling everyone.

There was a cheer of astonishment.

Marv climbed into the back and held out a hand to help Tuesday in, and everyone made room for Promise to clamber in too.

Leon radioed ahead to say they were on their way home. And the truck began its perilous journey, skidding and swerving over the snowy ice, winding its way toward the Isle of Bears.

And that was how they made it home. Back to an island where bears roam freely, a place where the dark can feel like forever. A place of secrets and mysteries. A place where a baby was taken from a frozen river and a marvel became legend.

The snow kept falling and the going was slow, but when a glimmer of sunrise showed itself at long last, the truck pulled up on the frozen beach. The island's long-lost daughter and the boy everyone had been out searching for had come home.

Chapter 16

THE ICE DAUGHTER

Indi stood shivering at the place where the land turns to sea, exhausted with worry.

Behind her were several Polar Patrol officers, stun guns loaded. Tuesday gave a terrified gasp when she saw this, but Leon put his arms around her. 'They only get involved if a bear's aggressive. There's nothing to worry about.'

Florian hopped down from the back of the truck, his feet almost numb of all feeling, and ran to speak with his aunt, who was head of Patrol.

Whatever he said, the men and woman lowered their guns and nodded in reluctant agreement. Then Indi flew toward the truck and Marv braced himself.

Indi might have slapped him. She might have deafened him with her screams. She might have grounded him for the rest of his young life. But she did none of these things. The sight of him well and safe took away all her anger. The sight of the beautiful brown girl clinging lovingly to the bear, took away all of her doubts. *There was a baby, and she found her way home.*

And she did a thing which motherhood forces all women to do. She found her courage. She climbed into the back of the truck, kissed and forgave her son, then took the girl into her open arms, still keeping a careful distance from the bear.

Tuesday had not grown up with a language of hugs, but she felt at once that she could trust Indi. There are just some things you can know without ever having to say them. So she let herself be led over the frost-dazzled beach, with Marv at her side and Promise closely behind her.

Dawn had broken, but the islanders were tense with lack of sleep and astonishment at the sight of the girl and the bear.

Tuesday felt the stare of Polar Patrol, the same way she'd felt the gaze of the audience nearly every night of her life. And she realized with an uneasy shiver, that this was the greatest act of all.

We have to fit in here boy. We have to try.

And silently she prayed to the distant stars that they would.

All along the edge of the beach islanders gathered or peered from windows, unsure of what to make of this astonishing spectacle. *The Marvel and the Myth.*

Tuesday felt the skin on her neck prickle. Behind her, Promise stopped dead in his tracks, huffing and shaking his snout. The little group paused. Tuesday turned into her bear, suddenly wondering if she'd been right to bring him here.

'It's OK boy. Just settle . . . settle.'

'There's too much of a crowd, we don't want to unnerve him,' Trucker warned, and Florian sprinted back up the beach to negotiate with the Polar Patrol and the islanders, until the crowd had all but melted away apart one solitary figure. A grand man still in his skates.

Marv realized Coach must have been out on the ice, searching the island's coast in case they came back a different way. He looked cold, but unusually happy.

He crunched toward them on his blades. 'I believe this is yours,' he said, in that soul-warming tone of his, holding out the white swan feather and ever so gently tucking it behind Tuesday's ear.

She let go of the breath she'd been holding and gave a little blink of thanks.

'To remind you of the amazing life you've lived,' Coach explained. 'And this is to welcome you home,' he continued, taking a yellowArctic poppy from his pocket and slipping delicately it behind her other ear.

Tuesday raised her face to him, her hood slipping back so her hair danced in the wind. It was still twisted with sequins. Florian watched in silence, a gloved hand pressed to his mouth. Marv saw his dad dart a glance at Florian and small nod of wonder pass between them. He supposed they were just as amazed by Tuesday's arrival as he was.

Tuesday found herself smiling; even though this island was unfamiliar, with its wooden houses and misty streetlights and watchful eyes, she felt as if she were crossing a bridge between her past and her future. A future that was bright as a winter's moon. And she moved toward that future in step with her beloved bear.

As the little procession wound their way through snowy streets, Marv pointed out the River Raven, the rising peak of Mount Maplewood, the distant gleam of the Lake Rarity, the lake that never thawed. Tuesday, who was still balanced on the thin blade of her skates, just gazed at him wide-eyed.

As they reached Marv's little wooden house, Mya flung the door open, her face tear-streaked and tired but smiling. 'Don't ever do that to me again!' she bellowed, whacking her brother hard on the arm. Then she stopped. 'Oh my God—Marv you did it . . . You found her . . . you really are a Marvel.'

Mya gaped at the girl in the snow leopard cloak and the enormous bear with his purple collar. A circus act on her doorstep. Then she flew out of the house and swept Tuesday into a hug. 'I'm so glad you escaped,' she gushed, and even though Tuesday was a little startled she found herself smiling.

'Why don't we go on inside, and you could leave Promise in the back yard?' suggested Indi, a little unsure of how to proceed.

Tuesday at once drew back, stepping away from Mya's grasp and leaning against Promise. She would not be without her bear. Coach laid a gentle hand on Tuesday's shoulder. 'Let's all stay in the garden then, and have some food. You must be starving!'

Everyone crowded into the Jacksons' tiny yard, Coach, Trucker, and Florian finding places to lean or stand. Marv perched on the old swing, Mya sat on the steps, Promise—after he had trampled over most of Indi's plants and eaten an apple core out of the bin— curled up on the snow like a huge white dragon and Tuesday snuggled up to him. It was quite a sight to behold.

Trucker built a huge fire to keep everyone from shivering half to death, though he noticed that Tuesday did not seem to feel the cold.

Indi and Leon began cooking up a storm, glancing out of the kitchen window at the child and the ice bear. For the bear had brought the wild into their garden.

Promise, it turned out, ate everything—even ice cream! But Tuesday found it hard to eat anything at all. All the foods were so new to her.

Trucker eventually called for Rae to come down and bring some deer meat. This was at least familiar to Tuesday. He stoked the roaring fire and set about cooking it for everyone.

When the noonday sun began to fade, Indi insisted Tuesday have a bath or put some fresh clothes on. But when Tuesday tried to cross the garden, she felt as if her bones were harnessed to Promise by invisible strings. In the end Mya had the idea of putting a bucket of warm water in the shed for Tuesday to wash in.

Once Tuesday was wrapped up in one of Mya's dressing gowns, her hair in a towel, she did feel surprisingly better, yet her body was sagging with tiredness, her back bruised from where Marv had knocked her down. It felt like a million years ago. Indi sat with her a while, carefully freeing sequins from Tuesday's knotted hair and trying to comb oil through it. Promise closed his docile eyes and as the sky became dappled with stars, Florian bolted the garden gate shut and put a little camp bed for Tuesday inside the shed. The shed was bigger than the sled-wagon, but so full of hockey kit, it was like she had slipped into someone else's life. Indi set up a portable heater, but it made Tuesday feel as if she were melting, so Coach and Florian built the fire closer to the shed instead, wedging snow around it.

Marv and Mya came out and offered Tuesday a box full of books, but she smiled forlornly. 'I never learned to read. . .'

'Oh don't worry, you're not missing much,' joked Marv, but the look on Tuesday's face silenced him. 'I mean I could teach you, it's not difficult,' he said, changing tack, and he stood up on his swollen feet, scrambled inside, and pulled *The Ice Daughter and Other Stories* off the shelf.

The garden went quiet around him. Even the hunting owls stopped to listen. The bear grunted in his slumber.

Once in an Arctic land in a time of dreamers' magic, there were a people made entirely of winter. Their bones were cut from glaciers, their hair the black blue of midnight rivers, and their souls were matched with the bears they protected.

Marv paused wondering if this was the right choice of book. He'd never actually read it, but he knew how it went. Tuesday stared at him with a tired happy face and he continued.

One of these warriors fell in love with a mortal, a simple man of the mountains and they soon had a child. The little girl did not feel the cold and she lived for twilight and snowflakes. But she looked entirely human.

The Ice Mother's soul was paired with a huge bear named Hunter, who eyed the little human hungrily.

So the Ice Mother kissed her babe goodbye and left her with the mortal father. 'Bring her to the river at the first snowfall,' the Ice Mother whispered, 'and she will always remain protected.'

The father agreed. He called the little girl Neve, meaning snow, and raised her in the mountains.

Everywhere little Neve went bears followed her and wolves came to play. She was drawn strangely to starlight and icicles, and when the lanterns shone on her, her hair was the blue-black of midnight.

The father soon married a mountain woman and had more children. Neve, or little Nevka, as they fondly called her, grew up in a big happy family and slowly the Ice Mother was forgotten.

Neve had a heart full of warmth and a cold glacial beauty. One night when she was sixteen, she went to fetch water from the river and instead gathered a bucket of moonlight.

The next night she heard singing, and gazed out to see a ring of bears, their snouts tipped to the northern sky.

On the third night Neve rushed to the river, drank the moonlight down, and smiled as her skin began to glow golden. She stepped into the circle of bears and boldly joined in the song. At once the bears rose onto their hind legs and Neve saw they were not just bears but people made of winter.

Neve never returned home, but lived with the Nevkians.

Her father was heartbroken.

At the first snowfall every year, he rushed to the river and waited and hoped, and sometimes in the river's frozen surface he saw the reflection of a beautiful girl and graceful queen bear, singing together as if their souls were one.

Marv took a breath to continue, but Mya put a finger to her lips and gestured to Tuesday, who had fallen into a soundless sleep.

Marv slipped the book under Tuesday's pillow and crept to bed, though he sat at his window a long while staring down at the bear in the garden, the girl asleep in the shed.

Something woke Tuesday. She didn't know what, and she sat up, a fog of confusion swirling around her.

The island. The river. The boy with the bear-scar. Had she really done it? Had she really escaped the carnival?

She crept out of the shed, needing to see the night sky. She was alone in the moonlit garden but for Promise and a sleepy-eyed Coach.

He and Florian were taking it in turns to sit in the garden and keep watch over Tuesday while she slept. It was too cold for any one person to be out all night, and even Coach, who all but lived at the ice rink, had borrowed Leon's biggest coat on top of his own. He sat in the glow of the fire, warming his hands through his gloves, sipping something steaming.

Tuesday pulled her cloak about her and tiptoed up to the steps. 'Would you like a drink?' Coach grinned, offering her some hot chocolate. Very hesitantly

Tuesday tried a sip. 'It's delicious,' she breathed, giving a giggle of surprise. Promise gave a disgruntled growl and rolled over.

'That boy you got there is ever so docile,' Coach said, gesturing at Promise.

'We've always been together,' Tuesday shrugged.

'Doesn't matter,' said Coach, 'you've got a real gift for calming him.'

Tuesday gave a shy little beam and she settled herself in the shadow of the tall, coat-bound man.

'You know, I almost had a run-in with a bear once,' Coach said in a low voice. Tuesday stared at him, her eyes wide with the expectation of a story. 'I was out on Lake Rarity, much later than I should have been. Bears don't often bother with the mountain—but this one did,' Coach began, his eyes glittering at the memory. 'That bear came out of the shadows in a mad fury. And I thought that was it. I knew I couldn't fight the bear, but I thrust my hockey sick at him anyway. He bit right through it.'

Tuesday hugged the hot chocolate mug to her. 'What happened?'

Coach gazed at her wistfully. 'I heard this strange singing and a woman emerged, almost out of the mist and called the bear away. Saved my life.'

Tuesday blinked at him with a soft wonder. 'Is that a real story, or another one of the ice myths?'

Coach chuckled warmly. 'It sure felt like a dream . . .' His voice had dipped low. 'I remember I was so grateful I reached out to her; she was colder than ice, but I held her and kept telling her "Thank you. Thank you." The next day I still thought it was a dream, only I had the broken stick. With teeth marks. I'll show you one day.'

'Did you ever see her again?'

Coach shook his head. 'Nope. Not yet, though I'm fairly sure she came back to the island . . . once at least.'

Tuesday sat with Coach a long while, telling little tales about her happier times in the carnival, listening to all the folklore of the island, the Nevkian myths, the mystery of Lake Rarity, and the true stories of people stranded by storms who eventually made the Isle of Bears their home.

'There's something magnetic about this place,' Coach explained. 'People come and go, but Islanders never leave for ever. I first came here on a hockey tour. There was no one else who looked like me back then; I was the only black person on the island. But the welcome I felt, the gratitude families had when I started turning the team around . . . I trained Florian, and before him Old Stoney. The man who saved Marv's life. And now I'm training the younger islanders. Hockey's been my whole life; it's all I've ever needed, but when the Jacksons turned up they felt like family.'

There was a pause in which Coach gazed at her, his

eyes misted with cold. 'And now you're here Tuesday, you can be part of that family too.' She smiled at him, and though neither of them could see it, in the light of the fire the silhouette of their sweeping brows and proud chins was the same.

The next morning Tuesday was awoken by a merry little breeze and a lick from her beloved bear. 'You're my whole world,' she breathed, scolding him gently as he roamed around the yard, chewing on old hockey sticks like a massive snowbound dog. Marv appeared on the steps and could not stop smiling at Promise. He was so much softer than a wild bear, his playful nature quite lovely to see.

'I was wondering,' said Coach, as they crowded around the little fire in the yard, eating porridge that Tuesday had made. 'How would you and Promise like to stay at the ice rink, just for a while, until we can figure something out?'

'I don't know what Patrol would make of that,' said Florian quietly.

'It's my rink,' Coach added, giving Florian a look that made Marv realize it didn't matter how old you were, Coach always had the authority.

'It won't be forever,' Coach assured the Jacksons. 'We'll let the island get used to Promise, then see if Trucker can fix up a shack in the forest, with the woods-folk—they don't mind bears. Or perhaps with time . . .

we can build something in my back garden. Let's see how we go.'

So off they all set for the ice rink, a little procession of friends, with a huge white bear at the back. The day was bright and clear as melted water, and Tuesday felt hopeful. She pulled off a mitten and laid her hand on Promise's side to steady his energy as they moved through Bearsville.

Folk kept a safe way back, but they waved to her fondly and Tuesday felt a little pulse of joy as she waved back.

Coach threw the rink doors open and Tuesday stepped into the presence of ice air, the atmosphere soothing her heart. Promise lumbered through behind her and everyone else tiptoed along in an awe-filled hush. There was something so riotously joyful about having a bear in an ice rink coffee shop. Mya couldn't stop giggling. Rae was cooler, but even she couldn't resist a gentle smile. Marv kept close to Tuesday, not wanting her to feel overwhelmed, and Coach kept a close eye on them over his shoulder.

Promise trotted here and sauntered there, mistakenly knocking a chair over. He had no sense of direction inside, pausing at the foot of the stairs, a look of bemusement crossing his face.

'Oh, he's not good with stairs,' Tuesday sighed.

'You go on ahead, sweetheart. Sure he'll follow when

he's ready.' Tuesday gave a merry little grin and headed for the rink.

They all watched Tuesday skate alone at first. Even though Marv had seen her perform from a distance, it still made him almost forget himself. Coach was on his feet gripping the Perspex the entire time.

There came a low rumbling moan and Tuesday glided to a breathtaking stop. Everyone drew back as Promise dragged himself reluctantly up the stairs and put a tentative paw on the ice.

'Come on boy, it's OK,' Tuesday chuckled, as if she were coaxing a house cat into the snow. Promise prowled toward her and went sprawling, his legs shooting out in opposite directions as he span toward her like a starfish.

The rink held its breath.

Tuesday laughed in delight and skated over. 'It's really smooth boy,' she chirped, cupping Promise's chin. 'Not like Arctic ice.'

Everyone chuckled.

Word had spread across the island that there was a bear at the rink and a few of the hockey team turned up, desperate to watch. Sol ran over to Marv and hugged him. 'I can't believe you did this. I can't believe she's here.'

Tuesday shyly skated over to say hello, and after a little time, when Promise seemed content, Marv and Sol, Mya and Rae put some hockey kit on and cautiously joined Tuesday and Promise on the ice. Coach had his skates on and was there beside her, a bright joy in his eyes.

By the end of the day Tuesday felt completely at ease, a sense of optimism and pride making her braver.

It was only Marv who noticed Kobi perched up high in the stands. There he sat gazing down, stone cold at Tuesday and Promise. He met Marv's eyes, gave a cool callous nod, then slunk away.

Marv pushed his uneasy thoughts away and tried to hold onto the fact that Kobi was just one person and Tuesday had an island and bear at her back.

Chapter 17

THAT IS HOW THEY LIVED

Tuesday and Promise managed to sleep the whole night, on top of a heap of blankets, near the open windows. Coach was there to keep them company, and they had all the ice and starlight and hot chocolate they needed. But it was a restless slumber, full of snatched dreams and fluttering fears.

When morning came, a tiny splinter of worry had wedged itself between Tuesday's bones.

Promise sat up on his haunches beside her and gave a wide, sharp-toothed yawn, huffing in ice air. Tuesday giggled sleepily. 'As long as you're OK, my darling,' she murmured, sinking into a soft white hug. He rose and stared at the open window, as if he longed for the kiss of the Arctic winds.

'I need to skate outside, on a lake, with real snow,' she said to Coach, her eyes bright and searching. Coach considered this a long while, then he took her small face in his hands, gentle as snowflakes, and nodded.

'I'll see if Trucker can drive you to Lake Rarity, while I go square it with Polar Patrol. We need to be a little bit careful.'

Tuesday's face became serious. 'What happens if Polar Patrol doesn't like it?'

Coach smiled fondly. 'You leave that to me.'

But Tuesday felt a shiver of worry. She had seen the polar bear jail from afar. She had glimpsed the cage. A cage with no room for a child.

'Can we go at night?' she asked, and Coach agreed.

🎄 🎄

They waited till the dark was deep and thick. Trucker arrived with his beaten-up truck and Florian, Marv, Tuesday, and Promise clambered in. Coach stood by the starry entrance of the rink and gave Tuesday a salute. 'I'll see you when you get back. There'll be hot chocolate waiting.' And she smiled then, so joyfully that Coach caught his breath.

The lake glowed eerie silver in the moonlight and Tuesday was suddenly darting out from the truck, fastening her skates, pirouetting around her bear as he pranced amongst the twirling snowflakes.

They can't keep from dancing thought Marv, as he watched Tuesday and her bear. Even without his skates

Promise was gruffly graceful in the strong grip of her hands.

The wind scattered the snow, clearing a little path for Marv to skate out to them. Promise yelped giddily, then bounded off, leaving Marv and Tuesday skating in a fast-turning circle.

Tuesday grabbed Marv's arms and he felt the air snatch at his skates, the speed of the motion lifting him, and he yelled out as suddenly his boots left the ice and he was flying. Flying!

'Hold on!' gasped Tuesday, leaning back into the turn, balancing Marv's weight against her own so that Marv's whole body was horizontal.

'I am!' he yelled, though he knew she wouldn't drop him. As they spun, the world disappeared, the ice and snow fell away, the seasons vanished; Tuesday was all Marv could see, a rising moon lighting the sky.

There was a swift sharp howl that rang through the night like a warning. Tuesday lowered Marv to the ice as a shadow appeared at the edge of the lake. 'It's just Trucker's dog Eden,' Marv explained, but Eden's eyes were luminously bright, her dark fur rising in hackles along her back.

'What's up girl?' said Trucker, his voice serious. She gave a long slow howl, and everyone peered about, Trucker reaching for his hunting rifle.

Promise, who was running a jaunty lap of the lake,

stopped and gave a low growl. Tuesday rushed to his side, fear on her face.

Is it a wild polar bear? Marv wondered, but then he heard sneering laughter and he frowned.

Trucker and Florian both stepped onto the lake.

Kobi Stone skated onto the ice. His clothes were slightly bedraggled—and where was his coat? It was freezing. Marv went still, but to his surprise Kobi kept his gaze low, hardly daring to look at anyone and Marv realized he wasn't alone.

A man with a wild look in his eyes dragged his feet to the edge of the lake. Old Stoney. Kobi's disgraced hockey hero-father. The man who had saved Marv's life, by shooting his bear. But it had been a while since Marv had last seen him, and he looked terrible. As if every good thing in his soul had soured.

'Hey there Old Stoney, what can we do for you?' asked Trucker, slowly strolling across the frozen lake. Old Stoney stepped onto the ice, sliding around with a chaos edged in danger.

'Have you all lost your minds?' he barked, turning on Florian. 'Letting a bear get this close to our children?'

He staggered toward Marv. 'You of all people should know what a disaster that can be.'

Eden growled, but Trucker laid a firm hand on her and she stilled.

'Now just a second Stoney, Polar Patrol are fully

aware of our location,' Florian began. But Old Stoney seized Kobi by the shoulder and pulled him roughly toward Tuesday.

'I tell you what miss,' he hissed, in a tone that made Marv's skin crawl. 'Move out the way and let my son Kobi dance with your bear. Then we'll see how peaceful he is.' Kobi's face was ashen.

Tuesday didn't flinch, even though the man's stale breath reeked of whiskey and he stank of sweat. She stood as tall as she could and spoke with the calm of a child raised with a bear. 'He only skates with me.'

Old Stoney spat in the snow.

Promise rose onto his hind legs, startling everyone but Tuesday. He laid his huge paws on Tuesday's shoulders, but she kept still and took the weight, leaning into him, trying to still his beating heart.

'Is that so?' Old Stoney jeered, shoving his own son so hard that he went careering across the lake, where Florian caught him.

'Out the way and I'll show you how it's done,' he hissed, pushing Tuesday aside and raising a fist at Promise.

'No!' Tuesday half screamed as Promise lunged, grabbing the man's whole arm and swinging him up into the air before flinging him down hard. The ice cracked. The air froze. Old Stoney wheezed triumphantly, a red patch blooming on the ice.

Marv stumbled back in dismay. Kobi covered his eyes with his hands.

'Oh Promise, no . . .' Tuesday breathed.

Because she knew how this ended. A cage with no room for a child.

Polar Patrol doesn't interfere unless the bear's aggressive.

'Marvel I have to . . . we have to go,' she began to stammer, pushing a wild-eyed Promise to the side of the lake and seizing her bag.

'Tuesday, don't go anywhere,' cut in Florian, who still had hold of a shaking Kobi. But Tuesday was already clambering off the lake.

'No,' urged Marv, skating after her.

Trucker grabbed Old Stoney by the shoulders and shook him. 'Get hold of yourself Stone! Think about Kobi for once.'

'Useless boy,' Old Stoney muttered.

Trucker struck him hard across the face. 'It's you who are useless. You don't deserve him.' Then he dragged him off the ice, reaching for his phone to alert Doctor Marilee.

'Tuesday, just wait!' cried Florian, as she vanished into the maple trees. 'We'll tell everyone what happened.' But Marv heard the shadow of doubt in his voice. And he fled after Tuesday.

She moved so quickly, her skates finding the little frozen stream that rolled down the mountain and joined the River Raven, and she shot down it faster than a shooting star, Promise plunging down beside her.

Trucker threw his keys to Florian. 'Take the truck. Go after her.'

Marv launched himself on to the ice and tried running down the mountain after her, tripping and stumbling, wrecking his blades as he went. He had never skated downhill at speed. Without hesitating, he stooped low and dived forward, determination carrying him toward Tuesday. But the stream was so slippery, his blade hit every rock; then Marv was losing balance and careening toward a huge boulder. He smashed into it, going over his ankle, yelling out in pain.

Someone grabbed him, pulled him sharply away from the boulder, righted his balance. Marv was amazed to find Kobi helping him. His eyes a little swollen, his face so ashamed that Marv put a hand out to him.

They were rivals—yes. But they were teammates too. Ice Bear Miracles. They looked out for one another.

'I'm sorry about my Dad,' Kobi spluttered, not meeting Marv's eye.

'Don't worry—just help me stop her,' gasped Marv, and the two boys zigzagged down the stream at breakneck speed, Marv biting back tears to ignore the stabbing pain in his ankle, as the girl in the white cloak sped along the River Raven toward the beach.

The wind gave a ghostly wail, whipping around them.

Marv felt his heart lurch.

She can't leave the island . . .

Behind them the truck spluttered and bumped slowly down Mount Maplewood, and with a burst of adrenalin Marv realized it wouldn't reach her in time. He and Kobi would have to stop her.

They shrieked onto the River Raven, their blades loose and battered, pounding the ice with a fearless speed that could only come from years of hockey. They didn't care which bones they might break, how bruised they might get; they kept their gaze on Tuesday the way they did the puck, and fled toward her.

Tuesday's heart was on fire. She half leaped, half tumbled, half soared over the frosted sand and sailed onto the sea ice like a ship into the water.

'Tuesday, wait!' Marv screamed.

'Yeah Tuesday, wait—I'll speak to Polar Patrol, tell them it was my Dad's fault,' Kobi cried.

For a moment Tuesday seemed drawn, torn, pulled in two directions. The comfort and warmth and community of the island. The Jacksons, the ice rink, Coach, and a future of starlit skating on enchanted lakes.

But the north wind tugged at her hair, and she tilted her head to the moon, gazing at all that lay ahead of her. The Northern Lights, the midnight ice and her bear. *You are my family.*

'I have to go. We have to leave,' she said to the night,

moonlight making her dark hair gleam midnight blue.

'Let me come with you,' begged Marv, reaching the sea ice and staggering toward her. She was six or seven feet from him. So close. The pain in his ankle drew tears to his eyes.

Kobi limped after him, a snapped blade on one of his skates making his foot drag. 'My dad's drunk, he's stupid. I'll vouch for you, say it wasn't the bear's fault.' Marv could have hugged Kobi.

Tuesday took a gliding step toward them. 'You can lie low at the rink, then move to the forest like Coach said,' Marv breathed.

Behind them a Polar Patrol truck pulled up on the beach and a few men and women filed out with stun guns.

'They won't hurt your bear. Not now he's on the sea ice,' cried Kobi.

'He isn't safe on the island,' Tuesday gasped, and somehow all of them knew it was true.

'But you'll come back?' Marv stuttered, trying not to cry. 'How will I find you?'

She gazed at Marv. 'Thank you for finding us,' she mouthed, tears streaming down her face. And then, as if on a whim: 'Look for me on the river at first snowfall. Like the story . . . I'll find you.'

Marv tried to stifle a sob.

Tuesday spun on the edge of her blades and she fled.

'Tuesday!' Marv bellowed. Snow fell from the sky, as if summoned by magic, her words echoing back on the wind.

I'll find you.

The boy with the moon-mark scar, and the boy with red hair both flew forward, Marv's ankle buckled and he crashed to the frozen sea calling her name. Kobi gathered Marv to him, checked he was OK, then lurched after her, balanced on one skate, the other foot glancing off the ice to give him speed.

Marv held his breath, his fists clenched. Somehow Kobi was gaining on her, reaching out grabbing at her dark curls, but Tuesday looped around him, her arms flying up like flames as she span away, a bolt of grace and power, her hair slipping through Kobi's fingers like silk. Kobi wobbled, his one skate trembled and he fell, calling out helplessly as Tuesday vanished after her bear.

Marv crawled across the ice to him, both of them weeping. Marv put an arm around Kobi and they called her name into the winter wind.

Tuesday closed her ears to them, listening instead to the rhythmic breath of her bear. Through the falling sleet they ran, through the mysterious dark with its swirling mists and gales. Through the storm they charged, half blinded by wet snow. Tuesday didn't care, her tears had marred her vision anyway; she skated with her feet and heart, Promise charging slightly ahead. Flying toward the place that was her true home, the uninhabited north.

She heard the rattle and screech of truck wheels far behind her. She heard Florian and Trucker calling her name, and she bit down hard on a long curl of hair, forcing herself onwards.

Perhaps they would settle in Greenland, the place Tuesday knew best, move between the scarce townships and seek out people who lived in the furthest reaches of the world. A people unintimidated by a child and a bear. *Either way we are free. No one can put Promise in a cage,* she told herself as they fled, trying to ignore the terrible pain in her chest, a splinter of an icicle trapped somewhere between her bones that would never quite thaw. But if she thought about it, if she let Marv and the Jacksons and Coach and the island and even Kobi into her mind, the sadness of it might kill her.

So she froze her mind against them. *Promise must live, he is my life.* She kept these words running through her mind with every step she took, and never had she felt them more deeply. Never had her love for him seemed more real, than the agony it brought to walk away from her own story, her island, her fairy tale. Her family.

Somewhere to the east, stage lights glittered darkly, and far away, almost in another life, came the yip and howl of huskies carried on the wind.

For one dreadful moment Tuesday considered going

back. But she thought of Gretta throwing the knife, the snowy grave of the mama bear, and she knew that if she went back that too might be Promise's fate.

She gathered her courage and skated on.

The stars assembled and spun apart above her, the night seeming to shrink and stretch, so Tuesday had no idea of time. A steady wind picked up at her back, carrying her along as lightly as winter blossom.

She was so tired. The very core of her bones was tired. Her heart was tired. Her mind was blank with exhaustion.

A sound sang out to her through the starry dark. A sound she could have followed forever. Promise stilled beside her and turned his head, giving a little grunt. Tuesday snapped back to herself and shook the snow out of her eyes. Far to the west was a circle of bears, all facing in to each other. Tuesday frowned at them uncertainly and a cloud darkened the moon. She rubbed her eyes and saw they were not bears, but people, grouped closely together, a travelling community of some kind.

For a moment Tuesday felt spellbound by them, then the strange song reached her again and she felt the sharp pull of it drawing her in and instinctively shot backwards, stumbling into Promise, breaking him out of his trance.

Whoever they were she did not wish to meet them

tonight.

They turned north and raced on. Tuesday's thoughts drifting to Marv.

I'll find you.

She swore to herself that she would. That one day she would seek out the boy with the bear-mark scar. She threw her head to the stars, paused to catch her gasping breath, and forced her voice out through her teeth. 'I will find him. I will.'

A mound of snow jarred her blade and she almost fell, but Promise lowered his huge head for her to lean on as she scrambled to her feet.

More snow came down in a whirl of screaming flurries, and Promise planted himself in front of Tuesday, blocking the cold from harming her.

When the journey seemed impossible, it was Promise who wrapped himself around Tuesday, cocooning her with fur so that she was guarded.

A bear protecting a girl.

A girl protecting a bear.

That is how they lived.

Somewhere off the coast of Canada in the deep and frozen north, is an island surrounded entirely by ice. It is not the kind of ice you will ever have known. It is luminous and strange, and there are lost things trapped forever inside in it. The fin of an orca. A baby's boot. The figurehead of a ship.

In late spring some of the ice melts, giving way to a cold and wondrous sea. And from May till August the ice is no more than a whisper, glimpsed in rare moments on the surface of the island's mysterious frost-glittered lake. But in autumn the sea begins to slow and freeze. And when the ice is at its thickest, when there is no chance of escape, that is when the bears come.

And every year upon this night, wherever it may fall, the islanders hold their breath waiting hopefully for their lost child to return.

There are many dark and light stories on an island like this, many sad happenings, and incredible escapes. Marv Jackson knew all about it. For the most remarkable thing about him was not the crescent moon scar that marked his face, but how he'd come to get it. A story that would live with him forever. It was the kind of tale that worked its way into even the toughest heart so that wherever Marv went on the island, he was known as the boy who never gave up hope. The kid who led a feral bear across the ice on the darkest night and found the island's lost girl.

The myth and the marvel.

There was nothing they could do but try and see the miracle of it. For each of the islanders knew in a way that they could never explain that she was out there

 222

somewhere. She may have become a creature of legend, a child of myth, a girl who danced with a bear. But those who had met her knew she was real.

For many years on November 7th—Marv's birthday—Trucker, Marv, and Kobi drove out to the place on the ice they had last seen her, and left a gift for a winter queen: a pair of beautiful white leather skates, in the hope that she would find them and know she was loved.

Coach left the light on outside the ice rink and the door slightly ajar, always, with a pan of hot chocolate warming on the stove, in case she came back, or any other wandering soul needed shelter. And sometimes on deepest winter nights, by morning the chocolate was gone. A set of bear prints leading to the door, accompanied by the tracks of someone tiptoeing on the point of their skates.

At first Coach had taken the loss like a grief as bad as Marv, yet he never seemed worried about Tuesday's safety, accepting that she was simply 'out there'. A girl on ice.

Then Kobi came to live with Coach. The red-haired boy had spent most of his young life at the rink anyway, but now for the first time, he knew warmth as well as the brightness of the cold.

Together as a community they looked after one another, told their stories around roaring fires, kept their hearts bright with hockey and winter starlight, skated all year on mysterious frost-glittered lakes and lived their lives alongside ice bears.

Marv always went to the river at first snowfall, armed with a burning torch. Sometimes he waited till midnight, gazing at his reflection, searching for a glimpse of something magical. Though all he ever saw was starlight.

Yet once on his eighteenth birthday he awoke to find a beautiful snow-child built in the garden, her hair carefully sculpted into curls, beside her a cub with two polished black stones for eyes. And his heart swelled with hope.

That is how they lived.

Many Winters Later

Winter sunshine kissed the frozen sea, and Marv moved slowly across the beach, crutch in hand to steady his limp. He angled his cap down, not to hide his scar— for this was the best thing about him—the thing that reminded him of the worst and best night of his life. But more to shield his eyes and grab a moment of peace.

Playing for the Canucks meant that Marv was a marvel of a different magic. A hockey star the fans and supporters and local families of Vancouver had welcomed into their hearts. Back on the island he was as adored as Florian had once been. Well, almost. . . If truth be known Florian was still a firm favourite, even though he was long retired and a scout now for the Canucks.

Marv loved his teammates as fiercely as he loved bears, and on the days they were winning, when the puck seemed to glide over the ice and into the net as if it were destiny, Marv had never known a greater joy. Everything else disappeared. *Almost everything.*

She was still his birthday and his bravest adventure. But with the slow ticking of time Marv had had to accept that she was gone. He knew this with his head. Not with his heart though—the heart, Marv had come to learn, had an enormous capacity for hope.

There were other little mysteries that he took as quiet proof that she was out there. A single page torn out of *The Ice Daughter and Other Stories* that had arrived at his home one Christmas. It had been posted by hand through the door with a single word on the envelope: Marvel.

Marv kept the page of the book in his wallet even now.

Another time nearly ten years ago, when Marv had made the journey over the frozen ice sheets with Trucker and Kobi to lay Tuesday's birthday skates in the snow, they found a small sprig of yellow Arctic poppies, waiting for them, like a gift from a mythical girl.

Kobi had kept them and given them to Coach right before Coach died. That was the last time Marv had made the journey. After that he and Kobi had been too busy with training to get the time, but Trucker and Leon still drove out faithfully every year.

Helped by Florian, Marv and Kobi had left the Isle of Bears a year apart. Both of them got to live out their childhood dreams. Both of them got to turn professional and play for NHL teams. Both of them got to be the miracle their hometown longed for. There was never any true rivalry between them again. Instead a brotherhood formed in the spaces where once there had been a void.

Once every hockey season, the two boys from the Isle of Bears would face each other on opposite teams in rinks all over North America. They would smile, embrace, high-five, rough play, and always, no matter where they were on the ice, be acutely aware of the time and space and distance between them, like two orbiting moons crossing the same galaxy. Nobody saw it, but before every game the boy with red hair, number eighteen, would shoot number seven a quick bright-eyed wink through the clear plastic that shielded their eyes. It spoke of a thousand things he would never say with words: I love you. I've got you. You're my family.

A snowflake whirled in front of him and Marv caught it on his fingers. It was years since he'd been home for a proper winter. Years since he'd waited in earnest for the first snowfall on the River Raven at nightfall, peering at its glassy surface, only ever seeing his own blurred face. Years since he'd dreamed of Tuesday.

But injury had taken him out for a few months. He leant deeply on his crutch giving a long, deep sigh; if it didn't heal in time for training all of this might be over . . .

He bit the edge of his lip trying not to think about it.

Coming home was wonderful, but tough as well. It was hard to see how the bears had declined, hard to see the worry on Indi's face as she fought to try and save them and make the island a haven for them. Hard to step back into the memories of his childhood.

He turned reluctantly away from the sea ice and began walking gingerly over the crunching snow, heading for home.

A sound came to him. The glide and slice of blades. Then that same swift sensation of being watched kicked in, and Marv glanced over his shoulder, expecting to see a dog or high-circling bird. The beach was almost empty; it was mid-afternoon but a dusky sunset was already colouring the sky. He turned the other way, peering at the treeline where the beach became forest.

But there was nothing.

He drew his coat around him, and began stumbling on when the sound came again, and he thought he heard singing. Marv whipped around, as fast as his ankle would let him turn. But it was just the lilting voice of the wind.

Twilight was falling fast now and he felt drawn to the frozen sea, though it was a mass of reflected grey cloud.

He stood still staring, unable to look away.

And then there was something, like a gathering of air,

as out of the wind skated a woman without a shadow. She was tall and thin, with dark wild curls that glinted midnight blue as the first flickers of starlight caught in her hair. Her back was perfectly straight the way figure skaters' often are. And the soaring grace of her almost knocked Marv over.

Who is she, out on the ice without a flame?

A cloud of sorrow seemed to hang over her, like the remnants of some terrible injury you couldn't see.

The woman slid to a stop, looking directly at him, her hand at her brow shielding her eyes. Marv gave ,gasp of breath.

I'll find you.

Her skin was the same brown as his own, her eyes endlessly deep, like the dark between stars. A spattering of silver claw marks gleamed on her arms. Something at her wrist caught his eye. It was faded purple, a small bracelet of some sort. Marv went completely still. *Promise's collar.* His mouth was dry and he knew then with a deep certainty that Promise was gone.

Marv took off his cap and eased toward her. Not too fast, he didn't want her to vanish, to become a dream once again. At the same moment, she began moving, slowly gliding to him, and he saw that behind her, instead of a shadow were three very real young feral bears, following her as if she were their queen.

Marv's heart suddenly leapt to life. It was her. It was

Tuesday and she was leading the bears to the island, finding safety in a melting landscape, making sure they didn't go hungry, giving them the freedom to roam somewhere they'd be cherished.

The world fell away, and she became everything. A rising moon, lighting every sky of every night of Marv's life. Time seemed not to matter. He was five. He was thirteen. He was thirty-one. In every moment, Tuesday was the North Star. The real Ice Bear Miracle. She was the reason you would step into a storm, cross a frozen river, face a creature that tried to kill you.

She was the light that made the dark wonderful.

'Marvel.' The name came to him on the wind, a joyous smile lighting up her face. Marv forgot his injury and ran toward her.

CERRIE BURNELL

Cerrie Burnell is a writer, actor, and former CBeebies presenter, who has in recent years made a name for herself as one of the most exciting new children's authors on the scene. Her picture book *Snowflakes* was performed at the Oxford Playhouse to great acclaim in 2016 and 'Harper', her young fiction series, has been set to music by the Liverpool Philharmonic Orchestra. *The Ice Bear Miracle* is her second book for middle grade readers.

ACKNOWLEDGEMENTS

What a wild, unstoppable adventure writing this story has been. Both beautiful and challenging. It has opened up a world of ice to me and made our winters wonderful. And I'm so enormously grateful to the super amazing team of creators, editors, dreamers and skaters who have helped me bring it into the world.

Huge heartfelt thanks go to: My wonderful, dedicated, tenacious agent Claire Wilson, who first believed in Marv and Tuesday. To my fantastic, serenely patient editor Clare Whitston, thank you for loving this journey. And to Jasmine Richards, whose wise, sharp insight and warmth made this story real.

An enormous glittering thank you to all the team at OUP. Hannah Penny I am so lucky to have you and your sparkling ideas! And to the glorious Sandra Dieckmann, thank you for working through the night to get the stunningly gorgeous cover finished moments before your own little bear cub arrived.

To everyone at Streatham ice rink who has welcomed us. Particular thanks to Scott van Slyck for advice on Canada. Harry Ward owner of south London's best skate shop, for patiently helping us lace up our skates. Jimmy Gardner, Kate Adamson, future hockey star Finlay Oates- number 11! And all the Ice Coaches who do a phenomenal job. Shout out to Werewolves of London for amazing inclusive ice hockey. And biggest love to my beautiful Amelie who has stepped fearlessly onto the ice—I am so proud of you.

So much love and gratitude to my family and friends, especially my parents and daughter. And all the other talented, courageous authors who I'm lucky enough to call friends. Thank you for inspiring me and lifting me up, especially Abi Elphinstone, Katie Webber and Ross Montgomery—now all you have to do is come skating with me!

Before I wrote The Ice Bear Miracle, I had never been to Canada, never owned a pair of ice skates, never seen an ice hockey match or a polar bear. But that's the magical thing about imagining—a gift we all have. Our dreams can lead us any anywhere, often on the most unexpected adventures. So I followed the story to the ice rink, watched a hockey game (what an astonishing, fast paced experience that was) took figure skating classes, which was equally terrifying and breath-taking. And I was lucky enough to visit winter-bright Canada and become completely spellbound.

I am yet to see a polar bear, but if like me you have fallen in love with Promise and want to help protect our fragile world you can find out more on the WWF website. https://support.wwf.org.uk/

And to you, the reader and the dreamer, thank you so much for choosing this story, I hope you will love it for many winters to come.

Love and snowflakes
Cerrie

Ready for more great stories? Try one of these...

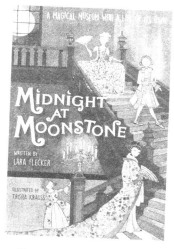